I0761458

A TERRIFYING BRUSH WITH OPTIMISM

new & selected

brian leung

SARABANDE BOOKS
LOUISVILLE, KENTUCKY

Copyright © 2025 Brian Leung
FIRST EDITION
All rights reserved.
No part of this book may be reproduced without written permission of the publisher.

Publisher's Cataloging-In-Publication Data
(Provided by Cassidy Cataloguing Services, Inc.).

Names: Leung, Brian, author.
Title: A terrifying brush with optimism : new & selected / Brian Leung.
Description: First edition. | Louisville, Kentucky : Sarabande Books, [2025]
Identifiers: ISBN: 978-1-956046-31-1 (paperback) | 978-1-956046-32-8 (ebook)
Subjects: LCSH: Sexual minorities--Fiction. | Families--Fiction. | Loss (Psychology)--Fiction. | Optimism--Fiction. | Seismology--Fiction. | Alcoholism--Fiction. | LCGFT: Short stories. | Novellas. | Essays. | BISAC: FICTION / Short Stories. | FICTION / LGBTQ+ / General. | FICTION / Family Life / General.
Classification: LCC: PS3612.E92 T47 2025 | DDC: 813/.6--dc23

Cover and interior by Danika Isdahl.

Printed in USA.
This book is printed on acid-free paper.
Sarabande Books is a nonprofit literary organization.

This project is supported in part by an award from the National Endowment for the Arts. The Kentucky Arts Council, the state arts agency, supports Sarabande Books with state tax dollars and federal funding from the National Endowment for the Arts.

For me, at last, with swans and songs. And for the tribes filling baskets in the darkest alleys and picnicking on the brightest hilltops.

contents

A TERRIFYING BRUSH
WITH OPTIMISM

NONFICTION

the seismology of *love and letters:* a guide to the ride?

I felt my first significant earthquake long before I fell in love or knew I'd someday become a writer. I was eleven and had grown up in San Diego County, all sage, no sand. The same way I understood that water flows downhill, I also implicitly knew that the ground shook from time to time. I hadn't yet, however, discovered boys, and being in love with one, being loved by one, wasn't a possibility I thought to even imagine. The night of that first earthquake I had fallen asleep in our living room on the tattered green La-Z-Boy that was the last remnant, besides me, of my mother and father's failed marriage. It was in the darkness of the early morning that I woke. The test pattern for a local station hummed on the television. My mother was working a graveyard shift at Denny's. My sisters were in bed. I did not know why I woke, but in seconds, the earth rumbled to life, the house shuddered and lurched. The shaking did not last long enough for me to be afraid, and when it stopped, I shut the television off and went to bed. Years later, another earthquake would wake me again, a stronger one.

I'm fresh from my MFA, but also thirty-three years old, at a writer's colony in upstate New York. A noted young bad boy of gay literature is baffled. "How can you not have heard of me?! Didn't they make you read gay literature in college?"

"Yes. Some."

"Then obviously nothing worthwhile."

It's fair to say that growing up I knew more about earthquakes than I did about love and letters. There were, to be sure, standard models in my personal life I might have turned to, my aunt and uncle, for instance, but with no ever-present parent in my house and decades before homosexuality was commercial and enjoyed pop-culture ubiquity, television was my teacher. I believed I was Fred Rogers's neighbor. I believed he liked me just the way I was, that he liked everyone just the way they were. Later, sometimes, years beyond his target demographic, I'd flip on the television for the comfort of his inclusivity.

One has to explore beyond the neighborhood eventually. The shifts going on inside me were tectonic. By puberty, I knew instantly it was men I preferred, exclusively. While my peers, boys and girls, were all "going together," and at least talking about being in love, I was alone. My first sexual crush was Kevin, the county bus driver, who drove the 49 route to the mall, and whom I dutifully waited for even though the 48 was a shorter trip. Kevin was in his mid-twenties, a long-haired blond with a thin mustache and stringy arms. He was my version of TV's Shaun Cassidy or Leif Garrett. I sat in the front of the bus and watched Kevin's big hands grip the steering wheel. Sometimes I'd fantasize that he'd ask me to mow his lawn and then invite me inside for lemonade. I knew we would be naked together then, but I couldn't imagine what, exactly, we would do. These were the first tremors of my sexuality, uncertain and awkward, and all of them about sex, whatever that was. And by then teachers were encouraging me to write, mainly praised my humor, my attention to heteronormative themes. I'd've saved myself a lot of time if I'd written about Kevin. Maybe if I'd been given James Baldwin's "The Outing."

It's seventh grade and I've written "Hike into Terror," praised and panned by my teacher as entertaining, but a too-dark depiction of family and marriage. "Too many murders."

That the earth moves beneath our feet has always astounded me. When we're out walking, we are floating at the same time on a crust of dirt over a magma sea—a planet pie of sorts. Once, when I was young, I lay on the ground, face up, eyes closed, to see if I could feel the subterranean movement. Nothing. But I knew the ground was moving, that I lived near where two tectonic plates meet. Their intersection creates the San Andreas Fault, causes the relatively frequent earthquakes and the slow drift northward of Southern California. In the year 16 million, San Francisco will be in Los Angeles's backyard.

That I understood from a young age, even at a remedial level, the workings of interior Earth amuses me now, for I could not detect the changes inside myself as I grew beyond puberty. I knew, for instance, that I was sexually attracted to men. I did not know I could do anything about it or even that the feeling wasn't considered normal. What a gesture it might have been had someone slipped me something by Edmund White or his contemporaries. I was simply floating over my teenage years, unaware that the friction of sexuality and the attendant inactivity was building up. It was lucky, I've speculated, that I was half Chinese, and that my father's traditional-Chinese-father child-rearing, even at long distance, caused me no end of anxiety that I wasn't Chinese enough. I was lucky we were poor, on food stamps for a while, that my mother entered into a third marriage with an alcoholic, annulled it after seven months, and then married again. White heterosexual homogeny was the least of my worries, the furthest thing away from what was my pen's mind happily writing entertaining fiction.

Before major quakes, there are sometimes warning temblors and I recognize those in the teenage version of myself. A knowing English teacher recommended, off the record, *The Color Purple.* My mother, hearing about the book's controversial status in high school libraries, insisted on reading it as well. When she finished, we talked, and as if she knew exactly what I should hear, she said, "It's not about lesbians. Shug knows Celie deserves to be loved." It was a generous moment that went over my head. That appendage was focused on all young men on whom I had crushes. Not the least of these was Ben, a naturally muscled, slim-bodied guy with a voice that sounded like an untuned guitar.

At a party at Ben's house I found him sitting in his parents' room with a group of other high school guys. Ben was lying on the bed surrounded by these jocks, hicks, and stoners. I jumped up behind him and unconsciously ran my fingers through his soft, thin hair. Though, surprisingly, there was not a single comment from Ben or his friends, their faces became varied combinations of widened eyes and contorted lips. If there could be such a thing as a silent avalanche bearing down upon you, it would feel something like that moment. I looked down and saw what my hands were doing and stopped.

I was aching and did not know it. I thought, at the time, I simply wanted friends. And for a long while in high school, that was true. I saw the popular people and wanted to be among them. Through design and device I achieved that goal but had no idea what to do with myself once I planted my flag on the rather tenuous soil of that new place. The geography, the altitude, was much different than down on the plains where I'd been a geek. But with Ben, and a couple of others, I understand now, I wanted to be in love.

*

I'm forty, established as a writer, enjoying a late lunch in San Francisco with a Baldwin scholar and a notable activist writer, both disgusted with my career. "Listen to her," he says. "You have to talk about what happened," she insists.

I have collaborated with him on some of his Baldwin scholarship, and yet, "I want you to write about us. I want you to write about the truth I am living."

Instead of love, I settled for a first kiss on my high school graduation night. Jeff was the editor of the yearbook, *Life*. I was the editor of the school newspaper, *The Horizon*, and the annual literary magazine, *Allusions*. Jeff had come out to me as bisexual earlier in the year, thinking, I suppose, I would reveal something about myself. Of course, I merely sat oblivious and still, wondering why he'd chosen to tell *me*. At our graduation party, given by one of the more popular kids and locked down by the parents, I found Jeff late in the evening. We ended up in the same tent, surrounded by five other young men. As we lay quietly in our respective sleeping bags, I reached out across what felt like an enormous fissure of space and grabbed his hand. He leaned into me and we kissed for a long time. The world did not rock, nor split beneath me. I simply felt good.

In the morning, I woke before everyone. I looked at Jeff, this person I'd kissed the night before. He was indeed male. I said to myself, literally, *Oh, I guess I'm gay*. To this day I don't even know how I collected that simple vocabulary. I gathered my things and smiled about my epiphany on the way home. Of course, I was still no closer to conceiving that it was possible for a man to be in love with a man. What I did understand was that it was possible for a man to kiss another man and that was the vein I planned to mine. One might hope such a person, a young writer, might have had the instinct to run to the bookstore or library to read about just what this gay thing was. Alas.

Seen on a seismologist's map, California is varicose with fault lines, the San Andreas a hardened artery that runs through two-thirds of the state. It is a visible landmark, a noticeable scar for most of its span, and many imagine it will be the source of the "big one." But there are dozens of less noticeable faults that the public largely ignores. In Southern California, seismologists warn us, fault lines striate the landscape, run under and through our cities. Not far from where I lived in Los Angeles, an active fault runs through downtown. In Hollywood, a block from the Capitol Records Building, a noticeable scarp buckles under the asphalt. We in the southern part of the state are more at risk, we're told, from these hidden faults than from the San Andreas, the tail of which trails off southeasterly into the California desert.

In those early years of my sexual activity, there was no model for monogamy, and the call for it, out of community self-preservation, had barely begun. Now, of course, monogamous same-gender relationships crop up frequently in popular culture, but when I was younger, sex was what gay men were good for and what we were good at, it seemed. It was what *I* was good at. It certainly never occurred to me that I and another man could be in love together, be safe together exclusively. Even now this is a difficult concept to explain to my heterosexual friends, that the possibility of falling in love didn't exist in my consciousness. The most understanding of them forget that all of us are products of cultural expectations and few, if any, escape that. A heterosexual assumes falling in love is possible because they've seen an entire human history of it. I should have known about and read Paul Monette.

I did what I thought I was supposed to do, despite the risks. I slept with many men, Travis among them, an ice-skating instructor, legs thick and brown as tree trunks, confident and graceful. He brought me to his bed but would not kiss me on the mouth. On the wall hung pictures of him and a male student in various poses. He took off his clothes and then mine. He was ten years older than me but seemed incredibly nervous. His hands trembled. He lay on me, his broad hairy chest warm and soft on my skin. At first it felt like we were two landmasses barely touching, but then it became more frictive, stressed. In minutes he had completed himself. It had been an entirely external event and he rolled over, staring at one of the photographs on the wall. "That's my ex," he said. "He left me."

"That's terrible," I said.

"I have AIDS," he half confessed, half blurted.

I thought instantly of his semen across my abdomen and chest. It did not have teeth, was not burrowing into me. Indeed, the house was not collapsing around us nor the world ending. This was not the "big one."

"That's okay," I finally said.

"You don't care? He did. That's why he left. I think he gave it to me. I never cheated on him once." Travis kept his arms at his sides. He reached for the television remote. "Oh," he said, setting it back down. "I'm not allowed." When I asked him why, he explained that his counselor told him not to watch television or read any kind of newspaper or magazine that might have reports about AIDS. Essentially, he was told to disconnect from the world. I was still thinking about the sex. It was my currency. Though it doesn't escape me now that mined salt was once a precious mineral for exchange.

The Earth bucks and boils beneath us, vents gases and steam, hot lava, disrupts, over time, the stability of its own surface. The manifestations of order we produce, our concrete and steel applications, our best-laid plans, are, as far as the Earth is concerned, only skin-deep. In the El Centro earthquake, a cross section of citrus trees in one grove shifted nineteen feet, row after row perfectly straight, then curved, a seismic doodle on the landscape.

In 1992, my boyfriend Roland and I attended an AIDS-awareness conversation at a private home. The house sat above Silver Lake Reservoir, a picturesque body of water surrounded by expensive homes atop a ring of hills thrust up by one of LA's minor faults. The community of Silver Lake itself was then, or had been, a place of bathhouses and leather bars, and where older gay men settled down after the faster-paced lifestyle of West Hollywood no longer suited them, the kind of sex they preferred or could procure.

Roland and I went to the meeting because, even then, we were unsure exactly what "safe sex" meant. Most of the others who attended were around our age, in their mid-twenties, all of us part of that fortunate generation that began our sexual careers before or in the midst of watching the previous one besieged by what was then commonly called "the gay cancer." It was not unusual, in those days, to see men in their thirties splotched purple with Kaposi's sarcoma or to know someone who'd gone in the hospital with *Pneumocystis* pneumonia. Sick men became, in their last months, bluish, downy haired, increasingly still as if involved in a process of lithification.

At one point late in the meeting, the oldest of the attendees spoke up. He was a handsome mustached man in his late thirties, a lemming that had somehow missed the cliff leaping. "Maybe you guys are too young to remember, but we used to have fun," he said. "We've been sitting here the whole time talking about safe sex. But I miss the old days. I liked the anonymity and I want it back."

I'm eight, maybe, and a big orange book is thrust in my lap, a big orange book with a loopy illustration of an elephant. It is read to me and I read it. Over and over: ". . . even though you can't see or hear them at all, / A person's a person no matter how small." Wow.

After the man, that lost soldier at the AIDS-prevention conversation, spoke, the room was quiet. Even the moderator remained silent. The very air seemed cleaved, all of us caught in a divergent boundary. On one side our past, the era of empowerment from living one's sexuality, on the other side a future, it seemed, of caution and blandness, the price of self-preservation. We were adrift, solitary beings. Because, in crisis, in epidemics, it seemed to me then, heterosexuals could turn to God, the Bible, and their love for a spouse, a girlfriend or boyfriend. But that was not part of our vocabulary. It could not be. All of us in that room, even the couples, were a community of single beings. Sex, not love, was our purpose, and without that, we'd lost our epicenter, the place from which all our energies emanated. We had no Bible. Perhaps someone might have pointed me to David and Jonathan or the work of Mark Doty.

During a college sophomore workshop a famous Southern California writer, feminist, and self-mythologizer dismisses my work. In the next class, when I mock her style with my angry reading of what I think is a duplicate of her writing, the reflection she wants, I end by slamming the paper on the desk and asking, "Is that it? Is that what you want?"

"Yes," she says, calmly, simply. "Yes."

The light goes on. She doesn't want me to be her. She wants me to care.

A year later, knowing I'm transformed, she nods at a piece of mine that will, a decade later, appear in my first book as "Fire Walk: An Old-Fashioned AIDS Story," and says, "Send it out."

By the day of the 6.7 Northridge quake hit, my boyfriend Tom and I had gotten serious. That is, we had moved in together after having met in a literature course. I was at the point where I wondered exactly where we were headed. I had in my mind even then, no role models, no pathway. My English courses had tickled over Wilde, dangled "Sonny's Blues," blushed with Stein and Forster sans *Maurice*, none of them, in fact, even remotely introduced as part of an LGBT cannon.

She pulls me out of a master's graduate seminar. "You have to write about this," she says, pointing to my story.

"Really?"

She is a notable Latina writer telling me my subject is about being half Chinese.

The Northridge quake had been the result of a blind thrust fault, which is to say the actual breach in the continuity of the earth was well below the surface. In this case, eleven miles underground, at 4:30 in the morning, the fault gave way. Tom and I were asleep in our apartment near downtown Los Angeles, twenty miles from the epicenter but hardly out of harm's way. At that point we had been together a little over a year, a time when I started wondering what we meant as a pair. Neither of us were dying lovers. We did not have the intensity of tragedy to bond us.

I woke just before the full force of earthquake struck. We lived in a bottom-floor apartment of a converted three-story house built in 1923. The windows rattled and the bed quivered as the main shock rolled toward us and then struck as if something huge, solid, had slammed into our building. Tom startled awake and rolled off the bed, pulling me with him, fearing the mirror hanging on the wall next to our bed would crash down on me. Plaster fell from the ceiling, our television and computer smashed to the ground. From the kitchen I heard dishes tossed from the cupboards. Outside, the windows of the upper floors broke out of their panes. The sound was intense, a mix of the deep, rumbling groan of the earth and the high-pitched whine of every manmade thing straining, if not outright breaking, under the pressure. I lay on top of Tom, the shaking so violent it put inches of air space between us with each bounce. I was sure at any moment the two stories above would come down on us. In seconds, it all stopped as quickly as it began, a few lingering pieces of glass falling to the ground just outside our front door, rimshots after a bad joke.

While Tom surveyed the damage to the apartment I stepped outside into the oddly dark morning. Our apartment was at the top of a hill overlooking much of Los Angeles and out to Hollywood. Few lights were on, and except for bleating car alarms, I'd never heard the city so still, never thought about the fact that traffic noise was not a sound indigenous to the natural landscape. But more than that, I thought about Tom and me. As we rode out the earthquake I had not been worried so much about my own safety, or his, nor any concern of our physical well-being. I worried, in those brief seconds of shaking, about what would happen to the couple that we were. We had become good together, something worth preserving. And as the earth shook us to what might easily have been the brink, I understood that the real tragedy would have been that two people in love would have been extinguished. And there it was, as plain as that. I was in love with Tom and the feeling was mutual. It was a strange realization, like trying on a new piece of clothing that fits you suspiciously well—there must be something wrong. But no, the feeling would not shake loose. There, suddenly, was that feeling I had never conceived of and I could speak its name. I had lived the lesson, not read about it.

At the Lambda Literary Awards: "Your writing's not gay enough." At a Modern Language Association Convention: "You're not Chinese enough. You shouldn't be writing about it."

After the Northridge earthquake, I discovered, the landscape I thought I understood suddenly heaved up, chock-a-block, familiar passages caved in, reliable landmarks upturned. Fidelity, for example, seemed anthropological, like an excavated antique lamp. What exactly does monogamy have to do with being in love with someone? But with all that uncertainty, I'd had my Elizabeth Bishop moment, "you are an *I*, / . . . / you are one of *them*." It was a final piece of the puzzle, that being in love, being loved, and not for the reasons one might suspect. Because what Tom was in love with, I understood, was not that I was gay, but all the parts of me that made a Brian, all the parts that would become subjects of my writing, my neighborhood of selves.

She reads it to me over the phone, the last phrase of the review: "First-timer Leung offers stories almost radical in their humane inclusiveness."

I am, by then, an English professor, know what I should say, but . . . "That's all Mr. Rogers," I tell her. And I mean it.

The earth shakes everywhere, trips us up, topples our houses and reroutes our streams. All of us, even in our stillest moments, are in constant motion whether we like it or not. The land carries us along, dips before our very eyes, or rises up. We are, in a way, parasites on its back that every so often get shaken off. From up here, on the surface, we convince ourselves of what is right for us and others, cling to the illusion of control, forgetting about the forces below, the inevitability of rupture and sudden shifts. But whether we pay attention or not, this is how things are. Just so, to each of us on an equal basis, if in different ways, through fissure and force, love and letters happen.

FICTION

all the presidents, men

We were young and had money. We loved each other, but we loved bodies more. On a typical week we spent three nights at the sex club. This was not a typical week. Marty added Thursday. He got to the club earlier than me because I had work. Marty liked to go hardcore right away, whereas I preferred to watch at first. Marty was undressed by 4:00 P.M. and getting a full Lincoln by 4:10. Later in the night, when he'd run out of takers, he'd let Deidra give him a Mary Todd, though he claimed he wasn't turned on by the whole transgender thing. I arrived at around 7:00, and after watching this and that group of Hands, having edged for a couple of hours, I found Marty. We discussed the new Hands we saw that night, and the old Hands that were getting boring. "Let's never be boring," he said.

"Right," I said, but what I meant was "I'm more afraid to be bored than be boring." We picked out the Hands we were willing to trick with at the end of the night, each of us nixing some of the other's choices. Too stubby. Too old. Too young. Too spotted. Too bony. Too hairless. But we settled on one, eventually, a new Hand with an oddly cropped thatch of black hair, and a body that was all lank. This is how we held things together, our agreement that no matter who or what, at the end of the night it was the two of us, a couple, Marty and Joe, and one other Hand. We had to do it this way because there were certain things in our relationship we could never give each other that we thought we got at the club. Marty's list was very concrete. Mine revolved around him not asking me for the things on his list. At 11:00 I was ready to call it quits for the night. The new Hand we picked out had eyed each of us and approved, though I hadn't seen him anywhere for an hour or so. I hadn't seen Marty either. I walked the entire dark complex, watching bodies enter and exit various doors and dark hallways lined with men giving and getting FDRs and JFKs. The only place left to check was the White House. Before I even entered, I heard Marty's familiar "Yeah! Do it." He was on his back, surrounded by naked erect men, including the new Hand that we were supposed to share. I'd never seen one, but Marty talked about wanting it, and the new Hand was giving it to him, a Millard Fillmore. "We're boring," I called into the room. "I'm bored." But nobody was listening.

first it's a lake, then it's a river

It was the fourth month of his return to addiction. He'd never been happier. His boyfriend didn't come back to him during his sobriety, but that was a good thing. That lying bastard. He took another drink and a quick drag from his cigarette. The lake was flat, lavender and black plum where the trees threw refracted silhouettes. Inside the cabin there were eleven guns on the bed. Should he throw them into the lake or use them for their intended purpose? He hadn't decided, and anyway, there was more bourbon and two unsmoked cigarettes. Time. But he'd have to make a decision. The protest in front of the courthouse was the next morning, 9:00 A.M.

She was firmly against abortion and faggots. One of her bumper stickers said so. She took a pill and recalled a favorite story about peeing into a faggot couple's chili before she brought it to their table at work. She amused her friends by using the word "sprinkles." From her kitchen window she saw that the lake was flat, lavender and black plum where the trees threw refracted silhouettes. She'd eaten in the kitchen because her dining room table was occupied by her recently deceased husband's guns, a baker's dozen. That lying bastard. Should she throw them into the lake or use them for their intended purpose? She hadn't decided, and anyway, there was her uniform to iron and she hadn't been online in over ten minutes. She took another pill. She'd have to make a decision. The protest in front of the courthouse was the next morning, 9:00 A.M.

They woke up to their alarms at 7:30 A.M., heads aching. The lake was pink and rippling. "Okay," he said to himself. "Okay," she said to herself.

Don't tell me you don't know how the rest goes.

six ways to jump off a bridge

Understand Blue Falls, how it got its name, how in dry years, in autumn, water slips over a flat edge, sheer and perfect, a wide liquid sheet reflecting a clear day—blue as an unraveling bolt of satin. But most years are not dry and most days are not completely blue. Not this morning, certainly, as Parker Cheung leans on the railing of the deck behind his home where he sees the falls and the observation bridge bisecting the line of water. Today is misty and the falls are loud, full after three days of rain. And there are people on the bridge. Parker counts four, one of them the sheriff, Katie Buckle. *Someone's gone and jumped again*, he says to himself. He takes a last drink of tea and walks inside, shaking his head.

Parker considers his dark living room, the *National Geographics* and *Reader's Digests* stacked everywhere, the mugs with their various levels of evaporating green tea. The answering machine in the corner blinks a single unchecked message. It could be his daughter, Susan, but he's afraid it won't be and so he's left it alone all morning trying not to think about it. Parker looks outside at the bridge, searching for the sheriff again. She'll be around soon to ask what he knows. At first he doesn't see her, but then she's back on the bridge, a brown-and-khaki thickness with a heavy walk. *Maybe I've still got time*, he thinks, turning to straighten the room, something he's still not used to even though it's been two years since his wife died. This was her part of their marriage, running the house, raising their daughter. He took care of the egg ranch, Cheung's Eggs "Something to Crow About!" But now that his wife is gone, he's shut down the business, and he hasn't spoken to his daughter in nine years. But there is the message on the machine that came while he was showering and it could be Susan. She might have remembered today would have been her mother's sixtieth birthday.

Parker starts by collecting the dirty cups, setting them in the already-full sink. He turns on the tap and hot water sputters out. The kitchen smells like fish, more so than usual, and he remembers last night's meal. He lifts the lid off a cast-iron pot, the head of a small red snapper offering a milky stare, a xylophone of bones strung behind. He throws the fish out the kitchen window and watches for a moment as three cats that he insists are not his fight over the carcass. Beyond them is the bridge from a slightly different angle. Everyone has left except the sheriff. She is facing away, toward the falls, resting both hands on the railing. *That's not the side people usually jump from*, Parker thinks. It's too close to the falls. The water isn't shallow enough for death and no one jumps off Blue Falls Bridge just to get seriously injured.

The first one to go over was Jason Glass. He was sixteen. Parker saw it, too. It was in the evening, he remembers, after dinner. They had steamed salmon dumplings and bok choy. He was full and walked out on the deck while his wife and daughter cleared the table. The night was cool and it now seems an important detail to him that it rained the next morning and didn't stop for three days. It was dusk and the bridge looked like something etched, a sequence of thick black lines. He saw someone pacing, not someone, actually, just a form moving back and forth. Finally the figure stopped, and a voice cracked through the twilight air, the form bolting across the bridge. It was running, yelling, "I'm Superman!" as it pushed off the rail.

Parker shuts off the water until there is just a small whining stream for rinsing. He starts with the silverware because that's how his wife had always done it. The water is warm, and the wetness makes his hands look almost young. He thinks again of the Glass boy. He has never forgotten the sound of Jason's body hitting the rocks, the solitary thump, barely a sound at all. Now, remembering, it is not important to him that he ran inside and startled Annie and Susan, could hardly produce words, nor that somehow he called the sheriff. It is the sound of Jason's body meeting ground, how his life ended as a whisper, in a riverbed, the almost powdery tenor of it as if the world couldn't care if he was a boy or a sack of flour. A reporter for the *Northwest Trader* asked him to describe what it was like to see the young man end his life. Parker watched the reporter's hand scribbling notes on a small pad. How could he describe a person's life dissolving into night air, the shocking lack of reverberation? He was quiet for a moment and the reporter stopped writing, his pencil a fraction of an inch from the paper. Finally, Parker spoke. "It's like reading a sentence and arriving at a comma with nothing after it."

Later, it turned out that Susan knew Jason. She was a year behind him in high school. In the four days before his funeral, she didn't go to class, she stayed home, took meals in her room where she and her mother talked for hours. Once, Parker heard her crying alone. He stopped and knocked on her door, but she didn't answer. "I just want you to know," he said, speaking into the wood frame, "there was nothing you could do. They're saying it was drugs. He was causing his parents a lot of trouble." She began crying louder and he put his hand on the doorknob but did not go in. Instead, he waited for his wife to get home.

Now, he has a message on the machine. There's no reason to think it's Susan except that it's his wife's birthday and no one ever calls. And why would she want to talk now after all these years? Parker isn't even sure of what he should say. There are ideas, forms of apology that sift through his mind nearly every day, but they all seem as vague as the reasons he and Susan stopped speaking in the first place.

As Parker washes the dishes, he keeps his eye on the sheriff. He watches her pace slowly as if she's trying to figure something out. But, as far as he's concerned, there's nothing to figure out. They should just tear down the bridge. Aren't six jumpers enough? Building it had seemed like a good idea at the time, but now Parker remembers when it first went up, and before that, too, when the chamber of commerce held a meeting in the VFW hall, well before Seattle had its Space Needle. There wasn't any reason to come to Washington then, unless you liked lumber, or perhaps cared to see the Columbia covered by a flotilla of logs. He remembers how Joe and Ruth Kent took a summer road trip in their Thunderbird and came back with pictures of gigantic concrete cows, the names of cities painted on their sides, invariably followed by a slogan beginning with "World's Greatest" or "World's Largest." Either that, or it was the home of something or the birthplace of someone. He recalls the chamber president passing around postcards and salt-and-pepper shakers the Kents bought, all of them bearing the name of a town. There was a picture of a huge ear of corn weighing down a pickup truck. From Las Vegas, they brought back a pair of plastic slot-machine shakers. They said Blue Falls needed an identity, a reason to come and spend money.

Parker feels the edge of a chipped cup and, for a moment, considers throwing it away, about as long, he thinks, as it took to decide on building the bridge. Parker remembers that was a dry year and everyone had fresh in their minds how simple and beautiful the falls were, how glassy and reflective. Everyone thought people would certainly drive to see them. Mildred Thomas was even smart enough to recommend they hire a photographer to take pictures before the bridge went up because that would be better for postcards. By then, Parker had only owned the egg ranch a few years, bought with money he inherited from his father, a purchase he knew he would never have approved of. His father never wanted Parker to do any manual labor.

With the last of the inheritance, Parker put up most of the money for the bridge and he remembers how everyone started calling him by his first name, or tried to. That was when he still wanted people to use his Chinese name, Pak. Only Annie called him Pak, and even she preferred her American name over Ling. He remembers she, too, wanted the bridge, even proposed to the chamber that they write Pat Boone to see if he would dedicate the bridge when it was done. Her accent was still so thick then he had to translate what she wanted.

We were all a mess, Parker thinks, searching the dishwater for any stray silverware, almost laughing. Pat Boone never wrote back, and Parker's wife stopped playing his records. Worse, though, after all the money invested in postcards and plaques made from diagonally cut pine limbs, no one could ever say for sure if even one extra person had come into town because of the bridge, though Parker did report he spotted a family on it one summer a couple of years after it opened. For about a week the people of Blue Falls allowed themselves to feel vindicated.

Now, forty years later, just as many people know it as Jumper's Bridge. Parker watches the sheriff tap her hand on the railing. It won't be long before she's knocking on his door.

The deeply stained bottom of one of the cups Parker has already washed gives him an excuse to turn his attention away from the window. He looks at the age spots on the back of one of his hands. *Old*, he thinks, returning his attention to the cup. He considers what he remembers about last night so he'll have it all straight for the sheriff, though he's sure there was nothing out of the ordinary. He wonders who jumped this time, what was the reason. Sometimes, you have connections with these people. Like Jason Glass. It wasn't until years later, months after Susan moved to Los Angeles for college, that Annie turned to him in bed one night, shook her head, and told him the truth. It had come out of nowhere. "Remember Jason Glass?" Her hair was still long and black then, just starting to show a few strands of white.

Parker nodded, a bit startled. He was halfway into a textbook on light therapy and he set it on his lap. "Of course, the one Susan knew."

"She his girlfriend. They fight over his drugs."

He didn't know what to think. "Why didn't one of you say something?" He looked at his wife. "I could have talked to her."

She sat up in bed, her face tightening. "No. You wouldn't. You always too busy with the egg ranch. That your problem. Always your problem."

His wife stayed mad at him for days, which seemed unreasonable to him. Susan had gotten over Jason, hadn't she? After the funeral she started working a few hours a week at the egg ranch as a candler. That first week, he'd asked her as she inspected the backlit eggs running by on a conveyer belt, "Are you okay?"

Susan did not look up from the eggs. "Fine, Pop."

"Good." Parker walked away. Now he thinks he should have said more. But she did seem fine, busy, occupied at least. And hadn't they later chosen a good career for Susan when she went away to study engineering? She'd even met a nice Chinese boy. At that point, at least, everything seemed okay. What more could they have done for her?

As he dries his hands, there's a knock at the door and he knows it's Katie. Parker goes to open it and catches a glimpse of himself in the dusty hallway mirror. He's still in his terry-cloth robe, the sleeves rolled up for the dishes. The thin rim of his white hair bristles out all over.

He greets Katie with a calm smile. "There's been another one, Parker."

He nods but does not invite her in. "I saw you over there." He and Katie go back a long way. When she was sixteen, working at the egg ranch was her first job. Parker made her an egg candler, too, but she complained after only a day about the boredom so he moved her to the chicken houses, gave her a boy's job to teach her a lesson. By the end of the summer, she'd become his best worker. It wasn't long before he had her supervising other employees, including Susan. Even though she's in her forties now, thicker, her blonde hair cropped long ago, it is not hard for him to believe this woman with the gun at her side is the same Katie.

"See anything?"

"Not this time," Parker says, looking beyond her to see what she's staring at. The ranch is wet and shiny, the spring weeds in his wife's old hyacinth bed bent from early-morning rain. "I really should get out here and do some yard work," he says, but there's no conviction in it. There would never have been flowers at all if not for Annie. He remembers how mad she was one year when she asked him to bring home lavender hyacinth bulbs—not the packaged kind, the bulk—so he could pick out good ones. The next year the whole bed came up white, though he swore he double-checked the bin label. Of course, he hadn't. It never mattered to him.

Katie shakes her head and scuffs a boot into the dark, wet ground. "Your cats are looking a bit scruffy."

"I don't claim them. They claim me."

"Not very smart cats," Katie says, turning around. "Doesn't seem right the way the place is all closed down."

"A man can't work all his life."

Katie smiles and takes off her plastic-covered hat. "You? Work?"

Stifling a smile and crossing his arms, Parker leans against the door frame. "As I remember, I spent most of my time picking up after you."

"Listen, you old coot. Gonna invite me in or not?"

Parker finally smiles and gestures her inside. "I suppose you're operating on that permanent warrant you keep telling me about."

She sits on the couch, lays her felt hat on a stack of *National Geographics*. "Jesus. So this is where the old-growth forests are ending up."

"Got 'em at Henderson's yard sale. I like to read."

"I remember. But your taste used to run a little more sophisticated. And Jesus. Do you read with night vision goggles?" She leans over and switches on a lamp.

Parker sits in his recliner, the arms so worn the wood frame shows in places. "Donated my books to the library." He sees the answering machine, the red light blinking over Katie's shoulder. "I can open the curtains."

As he gets up, Katie says, "I've seen enough of the bridge, thank you."

It is dark in here, Parker thinks, turning on a reading light. It casts Katie's face in a dim yellow, accentuating the wrinkles around her eyes. He measures her expression. She's not smiling anymore. "Was it bad?"

"It's always bad. But this time the body floated downstream and some kids found it." She pauses and leans forward. "Anything unusual at all last night? No lights? Voices?"

He had gone to bed early, had lain awake a long time thinking about Annie, about the next day being her birthday, and he was a bit ashamed he remembered the occasion now that she was gone. When she was alive, their daughter had to remind him almost every year. He recalls being awake long enough to watch the moonlight shift across the room, long enough to notice the clouds roll in. He'd fallen asleep to the sound of rain. "Nothing," he says, glancing again at the answering machine.

"This guy didn't leave a car or a bike or anything. He went out of his way to get to the bridge. We're just trying to make sure he jumped on his own."

"Maybe he isn't a jumper at all," Parker says. "Just some unlucky guy who fell in."

Katie has already started shaking her head. "I'd like to think that, too, but he's pretty bashed up and we can see where he hit. Headfirst. Left half his skull behind."

"Local?"

"No ID. But he was wearing a hunting vest and work boots, so he's from not too far."

"I don't understand how they get so crazy." Ed Cane had gone over something like this, Parker remembers. Got fired from his job as a welder at the Bonneville Dam three weeks after his wife and kids moved away to Idaho. He just drove out to the bridge, weighed down his pink slip and divorce papers under a rock, and jumped. It was summer and hot and everything smelled like burnt pine. Parker had gone out for firecrackers for the Fourth of July picnic. When he came home, Annie rushed out to the truck to tell him. One of the workers saw Ed jump. Said he stood on the rail, shrugged, and dove straight as a pencil.

Katie checks her watch. "You got any coffee, Parker?"

"Just instant."

Parker begins to get up but Katie stops him. "I'll hunt around for it," she says.

He listens as Katie fills the kettle with water, opens the cupboards and drawers, looks for coffee, sugar, and a spoon. He could easily tell her where to look, but he likes the sound of someone else in the kitchen. Annie had always risen a half hour before him and he sometimes stayed in bed just to listen. Even when Susan was born, he didn't mind the sound of her crying late at night. It was what made the house alive, these sounds coming from upstairs or somewhere down the hall, the comfort of hearing his daughter brushing her hair, the repetitive wisp of it, and the early clack of pans and breakfast dishes, how he could tell just by sound, before he left their room, whether they were having eggs or pancakes, sausage or bacon.

Even in those later years before Susan left for college, when they rarely spoke, Parker could listen to the house and somehow that was enough. How many times had he come inside from work and heard Susan playing too-loud music in her room and said nothing? Now he's beginning to believe that was a mistake, to be the father without a voice. Today, the answering machine blinks silently in front of him while Katie rummages around the kitchen and Parker is still looking for words. If it's Susan, he hopes she's left a number. Twice he's hired people to find her in Los Angeles. Parker waits until he thinks Katie is done. "Find everything?"

"Just fine," she says from the kitchen. "Maybe they just need a little hope, Parker."

"That's not it. Hope means you know you're missing something." *It's more about understanding the lack of something than the possibility*, he thinks. After Annie started sleeping in Susan's old bedroom, he believed for a long time she would think better of it and return. But she stayed there, died in that room, too, during her sleep.

Katie sits again, holding her coffee with two hands. "In a way, Parker, I think you're worse off than the rest of us. You've actually seen it happen. The Glass boy before I was sheriff, and the Silva girl."

"That was awful," Parker says. Of all of them, Rebecca Silva's death bothered him and Annie most. She was just twenty-three, the same age as Susan. The jump first looked like an accident, but later, her parents found a note. Her father was a Baptist minister in Tacoma. The newspaper photo pictured her as fair skinned, with red hair and a wide smile that showed only upper teeth. The story reported she was three months pregnant. Parker saw her sitting on the rail. She was wearing a white sweater and jeans. It was a late afternoon in autumn. The falls were beautiful and though he was concerned at first, he thought she looked relaxed because she was swinging her feet staring at the water. Suddenly, she leaned backward and was gone. "Annie was upset for a long time over that one," Parker says. "She wanted us to move after it happened."

"I remember. She went around trying to get people to tear down the bridge, too."

Parker looks at Katie, surprised. "I didn't know that."

"Oh sure. After the Silva girl, Annie tried to convince anyone who'd listen that we should wrap some explosives around the braces and blow it up."

"She had a point." Parker wonders, though, if it was really the bridge she was concerned with. When the Silva girl jumped, Annie was already upset because things were going badly with Susan. She had quit school. There had been a letter, a note really. Parker even recalls the color of the ink, a thick green that soaked into the open spaces in her handwriting. It said, *Dear Mom, I'm leaving school. I can't be an engineer. All I've learned is how nothing lasts.* The next day, Rebecca Silva jumped, and Annie was on the phone with Susan, crying, making plans to fly to Los Angeles.

Katie sets down her coffee and walks to the long curtains covering the sliding glass doors. She pulls the cord and they shimmy open, gray light wedging in with each pull. She steps outside onto the deck. Mist has settled among the tops of the pines. It makes Parker think of altitude, as if they are much higher than they are, as if his house is on some elevated precipice.

Parker walks outside, tying his robe tightly around his waist as Katie lights a cigarette. The falls are percussive and the sun, a disk beyond the clouds, silvers the bridge. "Sometimes it can be beautiful."

"That's the bitch of it. It's not the bridge." Katie crushes out her barely smoked cigarette. "It's just where they decide to stop being alone. That jump begins a long time before they make it out here."

"I can't figure why they don't snap out of it when they look down at the rocks." As Parker says this, he remembers that Jason Glass had gone over in the night and Rebecca went backward. They didn't see where they were falling. What does that feel like, he wonders, the few seconds of going somewhere else before meeting the ground? And what if there is even one synapse of regret, a spark of mistake?

"You need anything else?" Parker says, the urge to check the message growing stronger.

"Guess not," Katie says. "I actually thought we could do it over the phone this time, but you didn't pick up."

"You called?"

"This morning. I left a message." Katie points inside. "See, it's blinking."

Parker hesitates. "I know," he says finally. "I thought it might be Susan. I was waiting until you left."

"Oh, I'm sorry, Parker. You two still haven't spoken?"

"She doesn't want to talk to me," Parker says. He catches the sharpness in his voice and takes a slow breath.

"Jesus. You can't let that crap go on forever."

"I don't even know where she is. The last time I spoke to her she told me not to call."

"All I know is that I've got Jacob off to college and Jamie still at home, and I couldn't live without either of them." Katie smiles and pokes Parker in the side. "Their father's a different story."

Parker does not smile back. He wants to tell Katie how the silence is his fault, how when Susan dropped out of school he would not speak to her. Annie wanted the two of them to go to Los Angeles together to bring Susan back, or at least make sure she was okay, but he refused to indulge her throwing her life away, refused to leave the egg ranch unattended. And he never spoke to Susan, kept a vague tab on her through his wife, but didn't even know her phone number. When Annie returned from LA, she moved into the other bedroom where she'd stayed for all those years. And when she died, he couldn't reach Susan, couldn't find her listed under the name of Cheung, not under any of the Cheungs he called. There had been the funeral, the white roses over the mahogany casket, everyone from town. He had hoped that somehow Susan would have found out, that his wife had made some plan. But no, there was that whole quiet service without her in the little wooden church he helped paint every five or six years. "That's why I don't sell the place," he tells Katie. "That's why I bought an answering machine."

But Katie is quiet for a few moments. "I'm just small potatoes, but I could call LA again for you."

"I don't think so. You already did what you could." Parker's voice is suddenly soft and resigned. "It's my mess."

Katie offers an understanding nod. "So, what am I going to do about all *this* mess? It's only every few years, but they may as well've jumped in the same week." The two of them stand silently for a moment. "Well," Katie says, pulling up on her belt, "I should get going. If you think of anything, I know you have the number." Parker walks her through the house. He stands on the front steps as she opens her car door. "Maybe this was the last one," he says.

"I'd like to think so," Katie says. "But there's more than six ways to jump off a bridge."

Parker listens to the snap of wet gravel as she pulls away. Then it is quiet except for a few sparrows quarreling in the trees. He looks at the three large chicken houses, still and long as docked ships. The old delivery truck with faded lettering and flat tires sits near the fence, two seasons of unpruned blackberry vines already overtaking the front bumper. It is all so different now, so hushed, no gurgle of chickens working through the tin buildings, no one walking around with cardboard flats or running one of the egg collectors, no one at all. Parker stopped that just after Annie died, laid off people he'd known longer than his own daughter.

He sits in his recliner and focuses on the answering machine's small red light. He watches until it begins to move in tiny circles. *This is what it comes to*, he thinks. It's not at all how he imagined this stage of his life when he first came to the United States with Annie and they started the business.

Parker takes a quieting breath and swivels around to face the open glass doors and looks out at the bridge. He closes his eyes but it is still there, only in his mind it is even clearer and the sound of Blue Falls becomes the sound of rain, becomes something even softer, the sound of a body dropping through the air. It is like some improvisation of wind. And there is Susan's face, tenuous as a thread of silk beaded with water, glistening, drops falling and again the sound of rain, something more, pushing off, letting go. Parker thinks that this is the sound of decision, what it's like to hear someone jump when not a word is spoken. It is not an act of abandonment. That happened long ago and it was mutual, and no one listened anyway. *No one notices unless we've made it all the way down*, he thinks. No one hears until we are completely quiet. Now Annie is gone and unless Susan calls, she's gone too. *All that ignored intuition*, Parker thinks, *those families of the people who jumped missed it completely, all that pointing to the spot on the rail where they jumped.* They got it all wrong because it happened well before that. When it comes to the final moment, it's already too late. *It started for Ed Cane when his family moved to Idaho*, Parker thinks, *and when Jason Glass didn't get relief from twenty bucks' worth of plastic bag slapped in his palm.* It started when Rebecca understood a fetus would be a punishment for the rest of her life. These are the irrevocable moments when we can't see we're already in midair, when we push our daughter so far away she is lost to us, and then our wife goes too and we are alone. Parker imagines a blue descent, mistakes peeling off his shoulders, and finally, in one simple trajectory, the lightness he'd sought after all that awkward navigation, the relief that surprises even him.

I've wondered all along, he thinks, *and suddenly I know that this is what it feels like when you're falling.*

undoing

One lived to tell the story.

Claude W. Huxley appeared in Mudlick wearing a double-breasted gray suit, a bowler, and a pencil mustache that curved along the shape of his wide upper lip. He was a thin man, pale, with a curiously purposeful gait. He spoke to no one at first, sitting alone for half a day in Mudlick Saloon drinking brandy laced with ginger he supplied from a red drawstring pouch. After three years of drought, the population of the town had dwindled to less than five hundred, so word got around quickly about the odd-looking stranger sitting on a stool in the saloon and darting his tongue into his drink like a hummingbird. Some suspected he'd come to stay at Joseph Colton's burned-down hotel and was too embarrassed to say so when he discovered the great black spot where the hotel had stood. Others figured him for a land speculator who'd arrived to cheat people out of their drought-ridden property. But by the afternoon, most were certain he was a cardsharp in wait. Word was sent to the trustees about the stranger and word was sent back: "If he matters to us, we'll sure matter to him." At 3:00, Huxley put speculation to rest. He pulled a gold watch from his pocket, checked it against the chime of the dull oak clock hanging above the bar, and walked outside right down the center of the dirt swath that was Main Street, a black leather attaché swinging at his side with each oddly confident stride.

It was January 1916, and like so many days in the previous three years, the sky was cloudless, the air so hot it was almost yellow. It hadn't rained since early December and even that had been barely enough to keep the dust down. In those days, the trustees, constituted of just three people, held their meetings on the loading dock in front of Mudlick Hay and Feed. Jarvis Smith, Parnell Gotley, and Thomas Morton conducted their meetings every Tuesday beginning at 2:45 in the afternoon. It was the time they set for making decisions about the things in Mudlick that needed doing, not doing, or undoing, most of which was justified as necessary for the future of Mudlick's children. They saw Huxley coming down the street, understood without asking that it was the mysterious little man they'd been sent word of. The trustees sat, as usual, hats on their knees, Smith and Morton on short wood stools, and Gotley, with his great weight, on a rickety bench that seemed, each week, on the verge of collapse.

Huxley arrived at the meeting precisely at 3:05. He stepped up and onto the dock, his leather heels lightly scuffing the wood flooring. Smelling of saloon and talcum, he took off his hat, revealing a sweaty, but neatly combed, head of dark-brown hair shiny as saddle leather. "Gentlemen," he said. "I understand that you three are in charge around here." The sound of his voice had the certainty and rush of a waterfall.

Pewter browed, Smith, described in both myth and true accounts as dangerously temperamental, was almost always the spokesperson for the trustees, and in those weeks his mood had gotten worse after his wife, frantic about the drought, spirited away their only child, Eleanor. "We won't parch up, Jarvis," she'd spat the night before she left. "I don't have the patience of your worthless land!" After that, there hadn't been much Smith cared to be bothered with, except perhaps the opportunity to emphasize that very point. Upon Huxley's query, Smith looked over his shoulder but did not turn on his stool to face him. "Your business?"

Gotley's face plumped red. "Whatever you're selling out of that black bag we don't want," he said, hooking one thumb on the strap of his bib overalls. In addition to the fact he owned both the Hay and Feed and the general store, Gotley's position as a trustee was assured by his ability to intuit Smith's opinion on a given matter.

"I see," Huxley said. "Then we've struck an agreement, gentlemen. Because I'm not selling anything out of this bag." He held up his attaché, placed a hand on the side, which, for seconds, silently beat like the wing of a butterfly. He met each man directly in the eyes, forecast invitation with a slim grin. "But you're right. I am selling something."

The three trustees looked at one another knowingly as Huxley continued. "Gentlemen, what I'm offering is life itself. The element that transforms common dirt into the beautiful red rose, the element that keeps us all from turning back into dust and blowing away." Huxley paused for effect, fluttering the digits of one hand toward the heat-glazed horizon. Smith, Morton, and Gotley were listening, but did not move. "I'm selling water, gentlemen, acres and acres of life-restoring water."

The men, at the mention of water, were instantly reminded of their unquenched condition. Smith turned on his stool, giving permission for the typically silent Morton to do the same. He removed his cowboy hat from his knee and placed it on his head, the confluence of the brim and crown clotted with a dark band of sweat. "There is no doubt, Mr. . . ." Smith looked at Huxley square in the eyes. "Your name again?"

"Claude W. Huxley." He held out his hand, but Smith didn't accept.

"Like I was saying, Mr. Huxley. There is no doubt we could use water around here. But if you're talking about some sort of scheme to pipe it in, or a drilling operation, we don't got the time, the money, nor the interest." It was Smith's daughter who had pumped out the first bucket of silted water indicating their well at its current depth was near dry. "Don't tell Mother," he warned, touching his daughter's dusty cheek. She smiled, revealing front teeth freshly crowned from her upper gum that he was pleased to observe because the previous pair had nearly rotted through before they came out. He patted her. "Tell you to wash your face, darlin', but . . ." They looked down at the bucket's contents, and she giggled.

"You misunderstand," Huxley said. He stepped closer to the group and set his hat on the railing. Out on the street and beyond, Mudlick baked under the unprecedented January heat, the whole of it fuzzed and wavering in the sun's refraction. The intense light itself seemed to generate a sound like the high note of a plucked guitar string, only thinner and unrelenting.

At the wide doorway of the Hay and Feed, a few men gathered to listen in on the conversation. As Huxley took note of the growing audience, Smith turned and sent them away with a single "Git."

Huxley unclasped his attaché. "Nothing in here for sale, gentlemen. These are samples," he said, producing three dark-brown ceramic flasks sealed with cork and varnished beeswax. He handed one to each of the trustees.

"That's more like it," Gotley said.

Smith shot him a look to keep him quiet. "Can't be drinking in the middle of the afternoon, Mr. Huxley."

"Church folk would have a fit if they saw the committee liquored up," Morton offered. A word from him was so rare that both Smith and Gotley turned in his direction. Anvil jawed and gray, Morton didn't, on the face of it, have the qualities typical of a trustee, except the one Smith appreciated most, a willingness to fall in line.

Smith shook his head and held out his unopened flask. "Can't accept it."

"Again, you misunderstand me, gentlemen. This is not spirits you hold in your hands. It's water. A true taste of the acres I've brought to Amarillo, Cheyenne, and Albuquerque."

The first to break off the wax and pull the cork from his flask, Smith sniffed the bottle, and then looked at Morton. "Not whiskey. Not arsenic. Guess we aren't about to be done under or done in. What do you say?" It wasn't so much Morton's approval being sought as his concurrence, though to the extent it could be said, Morton was the closest thing Smith had to a confidant. It was Morton who had sat on the steps outside Smith's home listening not to the bullying trustee familiar to much of Mudlick, but to a father implacably distraught at his wife's removal of their daughter. "My little girl," Smith had whispered over and over, face pressed into his hands.

Putting the bottle to his lips, its neck hidden by his salt-and-pepper mustache, Smith took a swig. Morton and Gotley followed.

"That's water alright," Gotley said, sounding almost disappointed.

Smith tapped the brown flask on his knee but didn't say a word. He took a second drink and swished the liquid around in his mouth as if testing it for imperfection. What he found was not a flaw, but rather, confirmation that the water wasn't local, that it left behind more of an impression of sweetness than sweetness itself.

"Indeed," Morton breathed out after a second, long, sample.

"That's because it never sat in some muddy old well," Huxley said, looking directly at Smith. "That water came straight out of the sky." Huxley leaned back on the railing, retrieving his hat, which he used to fan his face, the forefinger and thumb of his unoccupied hand pinching sweat from his thin mustache. "I'm a bona fide rainmaker, gentlemen. And you just drank the proof. The very thing to restore our children." He continued to speak, but Smith's thoughts had turned to Eleanor and what she might be doing just then. His wife had sent little word, had ended her last letter with the odd missive, *Eleanor is now quenched, Jarvis. Quite.*

Smith brought himself back to the moment as Huxley proceeded through his presentation. From his attaché, he produced official-looking recommendations and yellowed news clippings—"HUXLEY DELIEVERS 5 INCHES," "RAINMAKER FILLS RESERVOIR." He said he'd come to Mudlick to do for the town what he'd done for those other places, bring rain. For $250 and $50 an inch, he promised to fill up every well and reservoir within a four-mile radius. "And I'll throw in that sad little mud spot you still call a lake." After so long without rain, the town's namesake, Mudlick Lake, had become a grassy plain centered by a shallow pond.

"I'd like to make it farther out," he said, "but my techniques to date limit me to a very specific area. Every drop of rain I produce will fall right here in Mudlick and within a reasonable perimeter." Most importantly and convincingly, except for a nominal amount of credit established at the general store, Huxley insisted he not be given a dime until he had delivered rain in the quantities promised. Anything short of this, he told the trustees, was free rain.

Smith leaned forward, skeptical. "Magic beans are never free, Mr. Huxley."

"Gentlemen . . .," Huxley began again, but Smith cut him off with a raised hand.

"That bread is already buttered," Smith said. He sat back in his chair and scratched his chin, once again looking down the length of Main Street, which right then had the same crisp and curl of a dead leaf. The place needed water. He needed his daughter. "Morton," he asked, still looking into town, "how many children total we got around here?"

Gotley's ripening expression beat Morton's calculation. "Three dozen," he said. "Give or take."

"Sounds about right." Smith sighed. More than anything he wished Eleanor was among their number. He missed her company at the dairy, had thought perhaps maybe someday she'd marry and he'd build her a place right on the property, a house big enough for grandchildren. But his wife was right. Without water it wasn't much of a place to raise a family. What child in Mudlick, he wondered, had any thoughts right then of staying in town once they got old enough and had another option presented to them? What would his daughter choose? Maybe she was happier away.

Two days after his meeting with the trustees, Huxley had erected a narrow platform thirty-five feet up in the three-pronged crown of a sycamore growing near a dry creek bed a mile and a half outside of town. Huxley had cut down all the branches higher than his platform and walled himself in with four wide sections of canvas tarp. In order to get up or down, he climbed a makeshift ladder constructed with wood slats pegged up the side of the tree every twelve inches.

On the morning of the third day, Mudlick was as hot and dry as the day before, and at that moment, perfectly windless. The only difference was a single white cloud-like column rising high into the bluing sky where it seemed to terminate in a pinpoint. Its source was Huxley's platform. Too white for smoke, too permanent for steam, the column was watched all day from the corners of the eyes of outwardly suspicious but secretly hopeful townspeople. When the breezes came, as they usually did in the late afternoon, the white line rising into the fiercely hot blue sky did not bend so much as bleed sideways in soft streaks, as if raked through by the hand of God.

People with the luxury of time, which was much of Mudlick—what crops there were had either withered or were so minimal as to not need much tending, and livestock had been reduced, in most cases, to the fewest possible animals—these people rode their horses out to see Huxley in his sycamore. Like wise men tracking the North Star, Huxley's curious visitors needed only follow the white plume rising from the narrow ravine where the self-proclaimed rainmaker had gone to work.

Even Jarvis Smith took time from his dairy to see what the man he'd hired was up to. He hadn't known what to expect from the strange little rainmaker, but throwing up a line of smoke, or steam, or whatever it was, into the begrudging heavens wasn't a promising start. The terms had been easy enough, it was true—nothing up front, payment by the inch—but Smith suddenly felt as if his reputation as a trustee was more on the line than if they'd mortgaged the entire town.

"Huxley," Smith called as he rode up. A pair of men in worn

square-toed boots sat below the sycamore drinking from canteens. Smith recognized them as the hatchet-banged Burton cousins, two young men on the verge of losing the small hay farm established by their grandparents. Any decent rain, and soon, would make the difference for the next generation of Burtons. "Huxley," Smith called out again to the canvas-covered square above him, where it wasn't hard to discern the sound of steady bubbling. "Jarvis Smith here."

Huxley hung his chin over the top of the canvas side. He'd shaved off his mustache, but his slicked-back hair remained as solidly in place as the day they met. "Sorry for the delay. People have been troubling me all day." The Burton cousins, clearly upset that Smith had gotten an answer when they hadn't, looked upward toward Huxley, whose face sat puppet-like on a canvas stage.

"Folks kind of want to know what you're doing up there," Smith said. He observed now that it was indeed smoke flowing into the sky, but of a quality dense as a geyser.

"Tell them I'm making rain."

Smith looked at the sky above the distinctly brown foothills surrounding them. Not a cloud to be seen, nothing except Huxley's white column and the sudden gray-brown flutter of a scrub jay skimming through Smith's field of vision. "Don't look like rain to me," he said.

Huxley climbed down the tree, his white undershirt soaked with sweat. He looked up at Smith, who remained on his horse. "Pardon my appearance," he said, dabbing himself with a surprisingly white handkerchief. "It's hot work up there in the laboratory."

"Laboratory": the word comforted Smith. In his lifetime a great many of the changes that made living easier had been born in laboratories. The great Mr. Edison worked in a laboratory. *The rain might come after all*, he thought, *and with it, Eleanor.* Smith's horse jostled beneath him. "I don't mean to disrupt your operations, Mr. Huxley," he said in a rare tone of apology, "but as a trustee I'm obligated to check in. Folks are worried that it looks like you haven't conjured much but a bit of smoke and"—he acknowledged Huxley's condition—"sweat."

"It's a process." Huxley laughed. "I haven't chanted yet."

At that, the Burtons looked at Smith and shook their heads. They stood, grumbling and brushing off the seats of their pants. "Got to head back," the older Burton said.

Smith slid off his horse and looked Huxley in the eyes. Thick boned and standing well over six feet, Smith towered over the little man. "When it was scientific sounding, the trustees thought we'd take a chance on you. But folks won't hold much stock in the idea of chanting. You got God-fearing townspeople worried about their daughters and sons, and I suspect you know that."

With Smith's face looming over his, Huxley cut him off. "That was a bit of ill-timed humor, I assure you." He held out both hands, palms up, each flushed pink. "I apologize. And as to your other point, I don't need Mudlick's confidence," he said. "All I need is payment in full when I deliver, which will be soon if I get back up to the laboratory."

"And all I need," Smith said, "is for you to get the thing done."

The Burton cousins, who'd slowed their exit, appeared skeptical. At least they'd seen him doing his job as a trustee, Smith thought, and in any case, he decided, may as well be hanged for a sheep as a lamb. "Git back to it," he said to Huxley.

The little man turned, the back of his shirt blotched with sweat, and then scrambled up the ladder that ran like an exterior spine along the trunk of the sycamore. Halfway up, he stopped and looked at Smith, who had returned to his horse. "If it helps," he smiled, "instead of chanting, call it praying."

Smith raised an eyebrow. "That's worse. Folks've already prayed a hole in the sky and haven't got a drop of rain to show for it." Smith straightened his horse to head back. He examined partially exposed roots of Huxley's sycamore protruding into the dry creek bed. He called back up to the rainmaker, who had already disappeared beyond the canvas walls of his platform. "If we get a gullywhumper like you promise, Huxley, I wouldn't stay perched up in that tree very long."

On the ride back, Smith found he didn't have much interest in heading into town, not to his dairy either, where during these dry days there wasn't but a fraction of the work to be done, and where the place seemed wholly empty without the sight of his daughter overloving her cat on the steps outside their home. Instead, he rode up a hill that offered a fairly good view of Mudlick's railroad tracks crossing the near-dry riverbed in the distance, and beyond that, a peek at the narrow valley where he'd started the dairy. It wasn't a landscape ever much favored with green, but instead, what the residents called green until maybe they caught sight of a shiny bolt of emerald cloth or some newly minted gadgetry that reminded them what the color really was. Now Mudlick looked to Smith like ash, the buildings fragile and tentative as remnant clumps from a cookstove's last fire.

He looked behind him where now, Huxley's column of smoke had been replaced by intermittent puffs as if it were Morse code rising slowly into the empty heavens. "Dear God." Smith sighed, and then caught himself. Huxley had mentioned prayer and here was the start of one announcing itself without a thought. Smith had never been one for churchgoing, but had been known to step into the Presbyterian services when it was called for. And now, something tugged at him. Eleanor was gone and in Huxley he'd put into motion a plan he hoped would return his daughter to him. But what was happening? Like no other time in his life, Smith felt hamstrung, wasn't sure if he was doing or undoing, or if there was a difference. Good intentions come with no warranty, he was beginning to understand. Again, he looked into the sky, but this time not at Huxley's white stitchery. Removing his hat, he pushed back against his anger and spoke as earnestly as he knew how. "Hope you're in a prayer-answering mood."

On the fifth day of Huxley's presence in Mudlick, in the lavender shades of twilight, the wind picked up and the sky began to cloud. By midnight, a fully-fledged storm was at work, the kind, even in rainy years, Mudlick seldom experienced. Residents woke to boils of thunder and heavy winds pelting the walls of their homes with debris. It rained all night and all the next day, and the next, each hour worse than the previous. It poured like it never had before. Creeks that Mudlick almost forgot had ever flowed spilled over their banks and filled the lake so fast it was triple its normal size. The small valley where Jarvis Smith ran his dairy flooded side to side, swallowed his already-thinned herd, and collapsed his barns. When it was clear his house was next, Smith got on his horse and rode through the downpour into town where he found Thomas Morton, his face half shaved, standing mud-soaked and dazed on the dock of the Hay and Feed. There was no sign of Parnell Gotley. "My place is flooded to the rafters," Morton said, speaking loud enough to be heard over the rain.

"The dairy went this morning," Smith said. "I won't have anything left." Visibility was terrible but the pair knew the lower half of Mudlick and well into the valley was underwater. Even the railroad trestle, Mudlick's artery to commerce, had washed out. Only the portion of town surrounding where Smith and Morton stood was elevated enough to keep from being washed away.

"In God's name, what brought this on us?" Morton asked.

Smith offered a steely glare. "Prayer," he said, and then, thinking of Huxley, "or the Devil himself." He pointed in the direction of where Huxley had set up operations, the site now hidden beyond a sogged gray fuzz of cloud and the sound of air-shattering rain. He confided to Morton about his moment on the hill when he'd looked to Heaven for help, offered up a prayer that he admitted came out of him somewhere between plea and lecture. And now, whether it was because of an answered prayer or whatever concoction Huxley sent into the sky, Mudlick had gotten more than it bargained for. But even as Smith thought it, he had a growing sense that when it came to him, it might be what he deserved, and that his Eleanor was slipping away for good.

"Think Huxley is still at it?" Morton asked. He squinted as if he might be able to make out some sign of the man they'd hired to bring rain.

"Suppose I ought to ride out along the hillsides and get him to stop. Serve him right if he's washed away already."

"Jarvis, you can't be risking your life like that. You got a daughter to think of."

"The situation needs undoing," Smith said. There was likely nothing to be done, he knew, but the illusion that there was might see Mudlick through a little while longer. He'd learned that people often paid just as much attention to action as they did results even if the former amounted to about as much as thumb twiddling. He took off his hat and tapped on the rain-darkened wood railing. "The trustees got us into this fix, and I'm head of the trustees. I have to go if it's the last thing I do for this town."

"Whoever said you're the head of the trustees?" Morton asked. There had never been an official distinction between the members. In reply, Smith tapped on his hat and looked at Morton in the eyes with a solid stare.

*

Morton told the story, which had its variations as years passed, but which always ended the same. He recalled standing on the loading dock of the Hay and Feed where the trustees held their meetings and where they'd given Claude W. Huxley permission to make rain. Just five days after that decision Smith was stepping off the loading dock to put an end to Huxley's work. When Smith reached the bottom of the steps, he halted, was enveloped by the battering rain, which made no difference because the brown length of him was already soaked through. "What's the matter?" Morton called.

Smith didn't turn but Morton made out what he'd said. "If it comes to it, tell Eleanor I love her."

"You'll tell her yourself." Morton tried to sound optimistic but he understood it was a hollow attempt. "You're Jarvis Smith. You'll find Huxley and turn off the sky. You're doing it for Eleanor. You're doing it for the children."

Now Smith turned and looked up at Morton, rain sliding off the brim of his hat, gray eyes focused. "We say that, Thomas, but we never really do anything for them." Smith mounted his horse without another word, did not look back as he rode off to save what was left of Mudlick. To his dying day, Morton described Smith's ride down Main Street becoming a silhouette of horse and rider fading in the rain, disappearing from bottom to top, submerging, all of Smith enveloped, except for his hat, which Morton said remained distinct for a long time, grew smaller, floated in the liquid air.

dog sleep

Su Yin had come over at my request. It was the first time she'd been back to the house since the day four months earlier when she filled the minivan with all her clothes, half the bedding, and the toaster oven. But we were working on it. The plan was for her to move back in when Gavin came home from school for the summer. We'd give it one last shot, the three of us a family again. The red lettering on our pagoda mailbox would be true, *The Han Family.*

We sat in the room on the very bed where we conceived Gavin. The air exchanger we'd fought over years earlier moaned in the attic, and our shar-pei, Ritchie, growled and twitched in his sleep in front of us. He was the reason I called Su Yin. This was Gavin's dog. Though we never talked about it, getting Ritchie was a substitute brother for him when we didn't have any more kids. I knew Su Yin would want me to tell her Ritchie was sick. He'd been acting odd for days, eating little, napping a lot. His sad face, more fold and flap than anything else, and his firm torso, made him look like a carnival prize gone wrong.

"He's thin," Su Yin said, bending down next to Ritchie.

She'd lost weight and let her hair grow and I wanted to compliment her but it came out wrong. "You are too," I said.

"I look fine." She rolled her eyes. "What are you feeding him?"

"Rice and lamb like always," I said. I smoothed a wrinkle from my shirt, a new blue oxford I'd bought that afternoon just for Su Yin's visit.

Su Yin stood on her knees, arms at her waist. People thought she was attractive, and she was. I met her in San Francisco at a mutual friend's wedding. She was the only one in pink and she barely spoke English. Su Yin was a Guilin girl, broad cheeked, more angular than most Chinese women. My family had come from outside Nanjing. We were short and rounded.

"How does his stool look?" Su Yin asked after watching Ritchie for a while.

"Jesus, I don't know. There's a yard full of it. Be my guest." I gestured broadly to the curtained glass doors and the balcony overlooking our overgrown lawn. I hoped she wouldn't take me up on my offer because she'd find I'd indeed let his shit build up for months.

Su Yin persisted. She put her hand on his head but he did not wake. "Have you taken his temperature?"

"I didn't . . ." I stopped myself from saying I didn't notice anything wrong until today.

"Of course you didn't." She shook the dog softly and called his name. He slowly rose and gave his stubby tail two meager wags, and then in a wet spurt, farted a rosette of bloody diarrhea onto the wall.

"This is just like with Gavin," Su Yin said. We were standing in our veterinarian's overly bright exam room waiting for her to come in. Ritchie lay between us on the stainless steel table. "There's another one," Su Yin said, swiping a paper towel at the brownish red mess drooling from Ritchie's anus. She'd gone through a third of a roll since we left the house. Even though she seemed to be keeping up, the dark, bitter smell floated around us. "How long has he been doing this?"

"Today. I mean, just since you saw it at the house." I sat on Dr. Mueller's chair and rolled myself against the wall, palms rubbing my eyes.

"Just like with Gavin," she said again. Our son had wrestled in high school. I took him to all his matches. He was a novelty in our town, a Chinese kid on the mats. But Gavin, always a roundish boy, constantly struggled to make weight. By his senior year he had slipped into a full-fledged eating disorder. When we sent him to therapy for a month, we told people he was at wrestling camp. His recovery over the last year was tenuous, and we both knew it.

"Ritchie was okay yesterday," I said. Su Yin bent over and kissed his forehead, her hair putting a shiny black curtain between me and them. Above her, on the wall, was a large poster advertising a drug for feline HIV. A healthy-looking Siamese sat over the caption, *Is he sick?*

"Always too busy. Do you know how many of my concerts you've been to since we married?" Su Yin paused as if I should answer but I knew better. She thrust her hand out showing three strong cellist fingers.

I couldn't argue with her, not even about Gavin. One doesn't choose to be oblivious. My own father never noticed that I was unhappy that he moved us from Hong Kong to Los Angeles. "I'm here with you and Ritchie now," I said, standing up and taking a place next to them.

Su Yin began to cry. She reached into her purse but didn't find what she was after. "What if it's too late?" She looked straight at me, her black eyes bleary with tears. We both turned to Ritchie who was sleeping again. His front paws were moving in the same oddly dainty way he liked to play with his sock toys.

The drive home from the vet was silent. Dr. Mueller told us that Ritchie was suffering from kidney and liver failure. I was relieved it was nothing I'd done. Common in shar-peis, she said. We'd return in the morning if we wanted to put him down. In the minivan, I sat in the back, Ritchie's head on my lap, Su Yin driving. I knew she would've preferred it the other way around, but she also had a thing about me driving her car. She'd had the seats recovered, I noticed, and the back windows were free from the glaze of Ritchie's drool and snot.

When we pulled up to the house, we didn't get out immediately. It was getting close to twilight. Su Yin sat, looking straight forward into the brownness of the garage door. I'd seen this view a hundred times with Gavin sitting next to me, still dirty and sweating from soccer or wrestling. I tried to picture where the trajectory of our family had veered. We'd checked off everything on the list like we were supposed to and still there I was, separated, with a reeking, dying dog on my lap.

I allowed Ritchie the deep sleep he seemed to be in, his muscles twitching now and then. I wondered what he could be dreaming about. I looked at Su Yin through the rearview mirror. "What are we going to tell Gavin?" I finally said.

"It's his decision." She waited a moment and then turned in the seat to face me. "We can't just put his dog to sleep without telling him."

The vet said that even though he didn't show it, Ritchie was in a lot of pain. She was surprised we didn't follow her advice and put him down right then. At that moment his sleep was partly due to medication. I thought of Gavin and Ritchie playing in the backyard. "It's such an American thing to have a dog," I said. "Back in our village, Papá let me have a pet chicken. We couldn't keep any pet that didn't take care of itself. I raised it from a chick. I called it Yinyin."

"We just had a fish tank," Su Yin said.

"After about a year, Papá killed the chicken and served it at a wedding."

I'm not sure what that meant to Su Yin, but she nodded her head as if I'd said something meaningful. "We're putting Ritchie to sleep in the morning. I'll call Gavin and tell him something."

"The truth?"

"I'll see what kind of mood he's in."

I nodded, and then repeated our objective in my mind. We

were putting Ritchie to sleep. It sounded odd to me, "sleep." He was already sleeping. We got out of the van and carried Ritchie into the kitchen, where we set up some bedding and where we could confine him so he didn't leak all over the house if he got up. But there was little chance of that. He was out of it.

After we got Ritchie settled, we each had a cup of tea, Su Yin leaning against the refrigerator facing him, me crouched on a slightly wobbly footstool. Su Yin kept her eyes on the dog, the steaming cup clutched near her chin.

"It's too bad he won't be around for the summer," I said.

Su Yin shook her head for a few seconds, softly clicking her tongue. "Gavin will understand."

"You can stay the night if you want."

She set down her cup and I began to stand but she put her hand out as if she was halting traffic. "I know I can," she said. "You sit with him for a while. Call me if he gets worse. I'm going home to call Gavin." She tapped my cheek, the first physical contact we'd had since we separated, but it didn't feel like love.

I listened as the front door softly clicked shut, and the minivan started up. It groaned in the driveway for minutes. I thought at first Su Yin was coming back in. I waited. Then I wondered if maybe she wanted me to go out to her. I got to the window in time to see her backing out, the headlights lancing the hedges as she curved away, my thin reflection appearing in the glass. I was overdressed. My new shirt came off first and I kept taking off clothes until I was down to my underwear and black socks.

I returned to the kitchen where Ritchie lay on his side, engulfed by the bedding as if he were a terra-cotta statue we'd half unpacked. His paws were moving again and he huffed a muted bark. I sat again on the stool trying to ignore the small paunch of my naked belly. I watched Ritchie for a long time, his eyes closed but twitching. He might have been dreaming about lots of things, a ball, a bird, a knock at the door. But I hoped he was dreaming about a time I could barely remember, when Su Yin was home and before Gavin got sick, when we sat in the backyard on lawn chairs and watched our son and Ritchie play tug-of-war with an old towel. I hoped he was dreaming about those times and I hoped he would keep dreaming all night, because in the morning, we'd go to the vet and put him to sleep. And we'd word it just that way because we never say what we really mean.

in case of an emergency, are you willing and able to perform the following functions?

His fingers are itchy. On a flight between Indianapolis and Las Vegas Markus Edell falls in love with a woman in the safety-information card in the seatback pocket. Markus is seriously considering popping the emergency exit in order for the occasion to meet her. The woman is heroic in her staid purple blouse and black skirt, appearing in the card not once, but twice, as she selflessly assists other passengers into a life raft, then, clearly, returns to the aircraft interior, rushing down the aisle to another exit where she assists passengers into the water. All this in sensible flats, sensible flats that match her blouse. That's okay. Markus doesn't like complicated women. Two-dimensional is perfect. He looks again at the emergency-exit latch. If he pops it she will come. He knows it. How many times have his friends blamed him for his loneliness, for not putting himself out there or being too rash once he does? The woman in the card with her not-so-tantalizing purple blouse will rescue him. He needs to be rescued. He deserves love. She deserves love. But now, who is this man in panel seven wearing a long-sleeved green shirt and khakis and being all too helpful? Will he come between Markus and the woman? Has he already? There are good reasons not to open the emergency exit when there's no emergency, and yet, that is what Markus is going to do, again.

some bones

It's not a crime in Tulkum County for an exhumed grave to come up empty, which is what happened when we got to Eleanore Verris's plot, or as we were obliged to record it, Number Seventeen. There was her limestone marker alright; the worn engraving said she was a beloved wife and mother and had lived from 1897 to 1926. On May 12 of her final year, or maybe the day before, someone had dug a hole into which Eleanore was to be lowered, and we'd dug one to lift her out, only, where her remains should have been, what we found was nothing but clay soil and about four or five inches of river stone. As it turned out, Number Eighteen, Number Nineteen, and Number Twenty-One, all Verris family members, were also without their human tenants. Aesop Verris's stone was Number Twenty, but it had no expiration date, just *January 10, 1874*, and the image of a squirrel hanging from a tree while extending an acorn to several smaller squirrels on the ground, the kind of tableau most every father constructs in his head. We didn't expect to find anything in Aesop's plot, but we dug anyway. It turns out there's something more interesting than graves with no bones, and that's a grave that has more bones than it's supposed to, which in this case meant none of Aesop's, as the investigation revealed, and instead, the remains of four other people if you relied merely on the skull count.

What does an unearthed pile of human bones look like? Not much, to be honest. At first, it's gray dots and stripes in black, musty soil. It's not until the site starts playing *Hamlet* with you and you're staring into empty eye sockets and a decaying grin that it hits you, hit us—widening the highway was going to be delayed until we got this sorted out. Setting the forensics aside—yes, they were indeed Verrises, and almost certainly Eleanore and her three children—what the *Weekly Upright* printed on May 11, 1926, was this:

> Death of a Wife
> Eleanore Ado Verris, wife of Reverend Aesop Thomas Verris, and mother to three previously deceased children, County Road 14, died on Monday, May 10, after a brief illness. She is survived by her husband but no known relatives. The private burial is arranged for May 12 at Whole Cloth Cemetery.

There is no record of why Reverend Aesop T. Verris never took up residence beneath his preordered headstone, and no explanation of why his and Eleanore's plots are separated by two children, with the fourth, a daughter named Abital Elizabeth, with a marked plot to Aesop's left, rather than alongside her siblings.

The reinterred Verris family, complete with Aesop's apocryphal stone, if not his remains, rest at a newly dedicated cemetery at the crest of a hill, which on a clear day offers a view all the way to the previous location. In late spring, fields of glimmering corn tassels reach upward, tall enough to conceal the highway that obliterated Whole Cloth. Each Verris—Abital, her two brothers, and Eleanore—got their own, if unadorned, casket. No claim was made that every bone made it out of the previous graves, nor that every piece of calcium phosphate made it into the right casket. There are twenty-seven bones in a human hand alone. And in this part of the country, it wouldn't have been unheard of for a finger or toe or a few teeth to go missing even in the youngest of living citizens. The highway needed expanding, so at some point we had to be satisfied with what we'd gathered and were more than likely leaving behind. Perhaps there is comfort in the thought that Eleanore may be at rest, at least in part, with all her children gathered around her in their own caskets. But in the weight of human concerns, nobody these days thinks about what might have happened to the Verris family and their patriarch. It was big news for a week or so, but folks have moved on, are agitated about highway maintenance and wondering just where their taxes are going if not to keep up the roads. We all complain about what matters to us most, which is generally what matters least.

world-famous love acts

Forgive my clairvoyance, sporadic and faulty as it is. I know we'll move on to other relationships after this, though none of them nearly as long or happy. "Goddamned flowers," you say as we pull away from your mother's house. "Tulips in spring. Black-eyed Susans in summer. Mums in fall." And I feel bad because we see her just once a year and you always end up fighting. We're only here in the summer, and it's certain there'll be an argument. The first one was about the fact she liked to put hard candy in with the brewing coffee, her own flavoring technique. The mint really wasn't bad at all. And then, two years ago, that silly thing over your father's clothes. Why not let her keep them in the attic? And this time, she still hasn't sold his car. You're upset that it's sitting at the corner of the soybean field facing the interstate, black and dull as a dead beetle, surrounded by window-tall weeds. "Nobody wants that old thing," she keeps saying. And I know what you're thinking: How could she ask just nineteen hundred dollars?

"You're too upset," I say as I wave back at your mother. "Sometimes I don't know you."

"Just be sure of yourself," you say, "and you'll know me."

This is our last road trip and we both know it, two men, one pair of jeans each, three T-shirts, and gym cards for showers. After this, it's all over, though neither of us is saying anything and it's not because the old Toyota is worn out, dented and oxidized from too much Los Angeles sun. These summer visits to Indiana are more a vacation for our car than us, the thunderstorms, the shade of maple trees instead of wispy shadows of palm fronds. We can afford another car but this is it. I can't be sure right now of why, nor even of our impulse to hit the road like this. Except that we've heard about a place in New Orleans where people have sex onstage and both of us have to see that. "Maybe they'll ask for volunteers from the audience," you say as we pull farther away from your mother's white farmhouse, the dust behind us caught in the sun like rolling flame as we shoot down the dirt road. "I think New Orleans is going to be very important for us."

I look at you with a question.

"Road trip." You shrug. "Like old times." And what you mean is that you're never happier than when there's a long stretch of asphalt and white lines ahead of you. For you, the point is not to see. The point is to go.

"I can't wait," I say, but you make it sound as if this is some sort of reunion. I understand what happens after reunions.

You have the road atlas open on your lap and I see the blue line stretching through Atlanta, down to Savannah, down to Orlando (can't we skip the Magic Kingdom?) and back across to Louisiana where nightly, we hear, people have sex in front of an audience while waitresses keep the drinks full and strong. But that's in a few days and right now we're making the L-turn and your mom's house is way off on the right. Way off. Small as a doll's house. The first place we ever had sex. That initial summer, the whim of me joining you on the road. Pasadena to Muncie straight through. And your mother putting me on the couch downstairs on the foldout, away from you upstairs in your old room. Her not-so-subtle hint about how badly the wood floors in the hall creak, how your dad just had to do something about them. The parental blockade was enough all by itself. Like a pro, you scooted along the banister, avoided the floor, and slid down to me. Our mutual embarrassment that this was our first time, and both of us in our mid-twenties and still saying we were bi. Even then you liked adventure. Think of the zucchini you brought from the kitchen. Then the missionary position. We used that one for a long time, but how long has it been since we did even that? Maybe on this trip.

I know it's on your mind too, though you pretend to be captivated by the house you are always so anxious to leave. "She's getting old," you say.

"Not really," I say, but you don't even notice I'm contradicting you. You just keep looking out the window. We turn onto the interstate.

"There it is." Your hand points out the window, teeters in the wind.

"We could buy it ourselves."

"I wouldn't give her the satisfaction." But I know you want it, the car. I know you're thinking about all the Sunday trips with you in the back seat and your dad and mom up front. How many times have you talked about your father sneezing the loudest sneeze you've ever heard and swerving into a cornfield, too proud to stop and back up? Your mother laughing as your dad made a wide U-turn, thunk-thunking through the stalks, the only version of a jungle you could conceive of back then.

We're passing it, the car, and maybe it isn't black as a beetle. I'm thinking instead of a dirty jelly bean, licorice flavored, a dull white *1,900* painted across its front window. Do you remember our first time in a car? That trip out to Barstow for your field tests. All those other seismologists, lesbians no less, and one of them having to share our room. But what a revelation. Okay, it was still the missionary position, but it was in a car. That, and the desert, that grayish blue of the evening, the cool we couldn't imagine would come after a day of one hundred plus. Nothing oral then, but we were good in that tiny space, both car doors open, room for our legs to hang outside. Afterward there was the swimming pool, a shard of blue in the darkness behind the motel. With us trying to be still in the center, bats flying by either side of us, skittering across the surface of the water as they drank. How could we go from that to being on the brink in nine years? I imagine the increments, the infatuation that wouldn't go away, the too-much sex that was still not enough for either of us, the driving around to estate sales on weekends while I started my furniture business, you in the passenger seat of that old van, helping me out, your day's wages: lunch or dinner and a quickie on one of the boulevards, in the parking lot of that lighting store, in the car wash. I think of those early forms of us then, and us now, and I wonder if this is how all couples end up.

We were close then. That's more important than you think. My sister told me about a man who called her in Des Moines. He explained that he was forty-seven. He had published thirty-three magazine articles and fourteen short stories that, added together, told exactly how old he was. He had also published seventy-four poems, the odd coincidence of being the mirror of his age. I'm sure my sister wasn't making this up. But this man said he was just plunking random numbers, and if it rang, he explained his situation like he did to my sister. At the end he said to her, "So, have you heard of me?"

Indianapolis isn't far off, a jagged lump on the bright horizon. That's the problem here, I think, the horizon. There are no landmarks. No hills to the east, ocean to the west. Nothing distinct. There's just this Midwest sun throwing down light like a wide-cast net. It's a shame the factory outlet on our left orients me, a row of brand-new empty business fronts.

"Would you want to touch anything that looked like that?" you ask, pointing at a radio-station billboard. *20 Big Ones in a Row!* it says above illustrations of the upper half of ten super-busted blonde women in striped bikinis.

"Those look like something you toss around the stands at a baseball game," I say.

"I'm going to count," you say. "I'm going to see if those bastards play twenty songs in an hour. And if they're one tit short, I'll complain." You turn on the radio, looking for the right station, passing up twang after twang until you think you've got it right. "That's a Cole Porter," I say. It's the Patti LuPone version of "Anything Goes."

"That can't be right. I don't see Cole Porter being endorsed by ten big-breasted women."

You shush me when I land on another station. "This is it." You take out a pen and make a mark on the corner of the road atlas. You really are going to count.

I guess we missed something because the disc jockey comes on after the song, laughing. So we spend the next hour listening to Van Halen, veering down and away from Indianapolis, Whitesnake, farther, Aerosmith, farther but you're keeping track even when our terrible radio starts to fuzz as we close in at the end of an hour. "Nineteen," you say. Metallica. "Twenty. They did it. Guess all those breasts didn't go to waste."

You turn off the radio and we're quiet for a short while. "What's this," you ask, holding up a small green brochure.

"Your mother gave it to me as an alternative to Sodom and Gomorrah."

You read. "Step inside Menno-Hof and begin your journey

where the Mennonites and Amish began theirs: a sixteenth-century European courtyard. Learn how a simple pitcher of water transformed a peace-loving people into the most hunted outlaws in all Europe."

"Where is it, anyway?" I ask.

"In Shipshewana. That's north." You fold up the brochure and toss it into the back seat.

"Anything down here to see?"

"I understand all the limestone for the Empire State Building came from Indiana. There's probably a big hole to look at." I know you aren't a tourist. That's it for you.

I like your new summer haircut. Or maybe I just like the idea that you did it without even asking me. I didn't even question the idea of going to New Orleans to watch people having sex onstage. Though, as much as I've progressed, I've never told you about Tijuana and the donkey show I've heard of. Now that I think of it, it was you who first wanted to try something beyond missionary. I have to give you credit. Back then I couldn't conceive of anything else.

It was the one-year anniversary of your job at Caltech. Twelve months of employment. Your apartment had gone art deco, half-oval sconces, the armoire I gave you for the new television and stereo, all that angular wood inlay, the picture frames changed. You even replaced the bleached-pine trim around the ceilings. Your bedroom all silver and gray. In the dim Los Angeles mornings we could almost believe we were living in black and white.

So that morning you woke up, twelve paychecks under your belt, a year to the day. You had money. We had money and we were happy. We started to make love on your bed the usual way but you stopped. "I want to try something new," you said. You took me outside to the patio, both of us naked and in full view of any other early-morning tenants. The air was heavy with the dusty smell of hibiscus, and the sun was little more than a vague pink theory beyond the foothills.

"What if we get caught?" I said, but you put your finger to my lips, and I remember that it smelled like maple syrup.

"We'll only get caught if you keep talking," you whispered. So we stood there, kissing, made love standing up, and your skin was warm on me in a different way, not the warmth of forced pressure, but something softer, the gaps between our bodies opening and closing allowing cool air to sift between us.

If you ever ask me how much I love you, I'd answer with this detail: When we stood on the patio making love, my feet never moved. I remember, because at one point I felt something wet and I looked down and saw a large snail tracing across the top of my foot. I endured its slow, unpleasant streak, let it be part of our moment so it wouldn't have to disrupt your fantasy. I was proud all morning of that silvery trail across my foot. It all seems so innocent now. We were just standing up, but we were equalized and that seemed right.

"I like a good snout," you say just outside Atlanta. No sex at the rest stop last night. Just a little sleep. We've been quiet since we woke and you're driving. "Yes," you say, "I like good snout. A healthy proboscis."

I'm not sure what brought this on, though I suspect the bloodhound in the back of a rust-pocked pickup truck in front of us. "On people?" I ask.

"Of course. I used to go in for small noses, but my tastes have definitely shifted."

I put my hand to my own nose. "And where does mine fit in?"

"I wasn't talking about you," you say, giving me a light punch in the shoulder.

I'm still feeling my nose. "But let's just say you are. What about it?"

You give me a good, hard look and then turn back to the road. Outside, the sumac is giving way to tall, straggly pines. It's a dry summer and the periphery is a whir of yellow green. "You don't have anything to worry about, Bit," you say. "Your nose is adequate."

Adequate. How do you get around a word like that? Especially after my old nickname. I never came up with one for you. You switch lanes and we pull up alongside of the dog and the pickup. It holds its head over the side, facing directly into the wind, ears and jowls flapping like brown socks on a clothesline. Its large black nose shines and flares slightly. I've heard that dogs like this can detect a particular scent in the tiniest fractions and I wonder if this dog is up there because the world is going through his nose at seventy miles an hour and he's just getting high.

"Would you consider rhinoplasty if I asked you?" you say.

"Would you ask me?"

"I suppose not."

I'm not surprised that this even comes up. We're both pretty vain. It's probably the reason we decided against the baby, if you could call it a decision. Both of us inexplicably depressed for months, having sex to fix it, doing it from the side too, by then, sharing top and bottom, and still we were depressed and then the baby idea, something to rally around. But it wasn't the adopting that brought us together. It was the decision not to.

I remember exactly. You lived on Mulholland Way, not Drive, we told people. Not where movie stars' homes overlook Los Angeles. We were below, where your address, 1940 Mulholland Way, had its own fame. You were right on the corner in that Spanish-style duplex that was all about curves, from the thick stucco to the arched windows and oak door. But the biggest curve wasn't part of the house. It was just up the street; on Friday and Saturday nights we got used to the fact that someone would come around too fast and not see how the road straightened out and smash into the wall.

The night we decided about the baby, the little girl in China we knew we could get, we were having angel-hair pasta with the fresh marinara I made from scratch in your kitchen. "We shouldn't accept it," you said. "Selfish people shouldn't have kids."

"We could get married," I said. "Kind of." And you just stared at me. I didn't think very clearly then. I made that whole dinner because I thought it would make things easier, the crabmeat cocktail, baked onion soup, endive salad, the pasta, the from-scratch breadsticks, and burnt-sugar cake. I don't think you ever noticed how I set the table, a water and wineglass, two main forks and napkin to the left of the plate, knives and spoon to the right, with the seafood fork angled into the spoon. All of it was proper. "We can't get married," you said, a bolt of pasta waiting at the end of your fork.

"Especially not for this reason. You just can't fake a family."

"It just seems logical."

"If you want to talk logical," you said, "get me some black pepper from the spouse rack."

I would have laughed, but instead I got you the pepper. Then you gave me the most direct look I've ever seen from you.

"You're the best person I know," you said. "I don't say that enough."

For once, I'd been the one who wanted it. And maybe you were right. What would we do now if we had a little Jella or Keena? It would be in school by now, bringing home paintings of lopsided houses and suns so close to the Earth they'd seem like predictions of the apocalypse. So, no baby, but we did make a commitment to be alone together for a very long time.

We're almost into Atlanta, the city itself. The morning sky is a bluish yellow, creased with thin clouds like wax paper wrinkles. It's already warm outside, slightly humid, and the air smells like bread, not cornbread—white bread. "Do you smell that?" I ask.

You keep one hand on the wheel and unroll the window. "Burning leaves?"

"Never mind," I say. "Should we stop anywhere?"

"Not unless Rhett and Scarlett are thumbing it on the side of the road."

I want to ask you if we can get out and walk around. I want to ask if we can just slow up a bit, if for once we wouldn't rush through. But I know what you're thinking: still morning, enough time to get to Savannah, press on. And so I flip my seat back. "Wake me when we get to Savannah," I say. But part of me wants to pick a fight to show how good a couple we are.

"Okay, Bit," you say and you wink. "I'll wake you if I see a good patch of kudzu."

I feel a poke in the side. "You want to see this?" you ask. "A bunch of Spanish moss and crap."

I sit up, roused at the tail end of a dream about our trip to Washington, DC. Outside we drive down a main road bordered by black-barked trees closing over us. The branches are necklaced with thick, dangling strands of grayish-green moss that slim to fine points. The houses on this stretch are broad porched, each painted a variation of white or yellow. The windows are curtained by material so thin you can almost see through the diamond-latticed windows. I unroll my window for a better look, and the heat whooshes in along with an almost unreal dampness. I immediately roll the window back up.

"Remember the squirrels?" I ask.

You laugh. "In DC?"

"I was dreaming about them." That was one of our first real road trips. It took us an hour to find a parking spot once we got into the city, and by then, as usual, you were ready to leave. But at least you let us stop at the Jefferson Memorial with its curve of not-yet-in-bloom cherry trees, one of them with a hollow trunk and a dozen or so dead, gutted squirrels strewn about, each with three heads-up pennies placed on the inside spine. At the base of the tree were nineteen dollar bills laid out end to end and a line of sixty pennies. Neither of us was even tempted to take the money. "That was our first dangerous sex," I say.

You think for a moment before saying anything. "Was that before the Transamerica building?"

"Yes," I say. That was a later road trip, a quickie to San Francisco and the unavoidable sex in the foggy night, up against the bracing of that building you called a "phallic wonder." We had a bottle of lube, so San Francisco had to be after. "DC was a year earlier," I say. "I'm sure of it."

"All I remember," you say, "is that you wouldn't go down on me in front of Jefferson."

"But all we had to do was step behind the statue and I was fine." Both of us laugh but I know you're laughing because these memories confirm your notions that I'm not as experimental, that I'm more puritan compared to you. Outside, the mossy canopy opens like the light end of a tunnel, and the bright sun flattens out the landscape. The refraction off glass and metal is startling, as if this newer part of Savannah is just moments away from combustion.

"Why don't we do anything like that anymore?" I say.

"We could," you offer, but there's no conviction behind it.

"Tonight?" I shuffle my feet a bit, sifting through candy wrappers and potato chip bags.

"Let's not plan it," you say. "It has to be spontaneous." And then, quick as a sniper on a tower, you change the subject. It's the kind of abruptness I can never get away with. "I thought we'd drive out to the Atlantic. We've never been."

We pass a sign that reads *Tybee Island.* I unroll the window for the smell of salt because I can tell we're getting close to the ocean. On either side of us are great stretches of tall grass ribboned with wide blue water where small boats leave temporary white scratches on the surface.

"Are you having a moment?" you ask and I know exactly what you're talking about, one of my clairvoyant spells.

"No," I say. "I'm just watching the boats. I haven't had a full-blown moment since Wallace." You mocked me a bit about that, just a bit. Wallace was giving me a ride in his new car when we got pulled over by LAPD. The whole time he and the cop were very polite to each other but I sensed something more. The cop was thinking, *Must be something up if this Black guy is driving a brand-new car.* And every time Wallace said, "Yes, officer," he was thinking, *Son of a bitch. I know what's up.* After Wallace signed the citation and we started back on the road I said, "It really sucks the way he treated you."

Wallace looked at me and said, "What way?"

"Hassling a Black man with a new car."

Wallace gave me a hard, corrective look. "I was going twenty miles over the speed limit," he said.

Later that night, when I told you all of this, you laughed. "You mean well," you said, patting my head like I was a child. "You've just got a little Sputnik inside you sending mysterious transmissions."

The oceanfront is obscured by rows of houses and summer rental units, but you find us a parking spot right next to a stairway to the beach. The air is surprisingly calm and though I can see the grass-freckled dunes, it seems too quiet to be close to the water. We walk along a wooden path to the peak of the dunes where a green-and-white sign tells us not to pick the sea oats—tall, thin grass rising from the squat dunes that looks like hair on a balding scalp. I tap you on the shoulder to see if you see what I see in the cleavage of a pair of small dunes: two men having sex.

You shake your head and pull me onward. "You'll have plenty of time for voyeurism in New Orleans."

At the end of the walk, the Atlantic spreads out before us. The bright, open sky and dark water come together like bolts of stacked linen. Suddenly you're taking off your sandals and running toward the water. I follow.

The water is surprisingly cool and timid around our ankles. The waves here are not like the Pacific. They seem tentative, weak pulses straggling toward shore. And not another person on the beach as far as I can see in both directions. Summer and this broad stretch of white sand with its band of darkness nearest the water, and no one enjoying it but us. I look up to the dunes but I can't see the two men, just a long line of beach fencing, wavy as the picked-clean bones of an eel.

You bury your feet just where the wave is deepest, where it feels like a last breath before retreating. "We've never stood right here," you say. You close your eyes and smile and I know not to say anything. New ground is important to you.

We've never been here before, it's true. We've never been to the Atlantic at all. Would I have ever been to London or Paris without you? Or New York and the closed-off subway terminal below the World Trade Center where you pushed me up against the wall and told me what to do? I learned to take orders then, listened carefully for where to put my hands, where to put my mouth. You taught me.

So I watch you now, jeans rolled up to your knees, speckled with water, white T-shirt glaring in the sun and still not as fine as your smile, the one I see so little now, and I know I still love you and I don't want to be done learning. I don't want this to be our last trip together, though I'm almost sure it is. I think we're seeing the end.

Florida is on fire. We saw it long before they diverted us away from continuing south, the hazy, brown smoke looking like a miles-wide waterfall defying gravity, flowing upward, the high-altitude winds scraping the top flat, making a river of smoke flow west. But I keep driving, unconcerned. In Los Angeles, these colors and wildfires mean it's fall. It's a ritual. The Santa Ana winds rush in like hungry gods, stroking the hillsides until they find someone with a match and a problem. And then we sacrifice, the whole city gathers around televisions to see how many homes will go up. And what's left behind are the sunsets, smoke-induced variations on amber. Browns and yellows you can't call brown and yellow, maybe cocoa, maybe the gold of Spanish coins. "LA's version of a rainbow," you once said.

They've diverted us west and the fire flanks us almost at the edge of the freeway. The smoke here is black, melting out of huge orange columns. An early red-white-and-blue campaign billboard stands just above the flames. There's a large photo of a jowly, pearly-haired man with unruly brows that dip over his eyes. *Rutch Hodgins Independent for US Senator.* Someone has spray painted over the *E* so that it reads *Sinator.*

"I read about that guy," you say. "He got married last year. She was nineteen and he was eighty." Then you growl and put your seat back and I know you are frustrated that there's so much traffic ahead of us, that we can't just go and be done with the fire. "When I was a child," you say, "my grandparents' house caught on fire a week before Christmas. They lost everything. And this is the part I never understand." You sit back up and look at me. "My grandparents came to stay with us and my parents took down the Christmas tree and put all the presents in the church donation box. All my dad said was 'No Christmas this year.'"

"Wow," I say, "you never told me that story before."

"Really? I thought we'd said everything to each other we could possibly say."

"Is that a good or bad thing?" I ask, just as we get beyond the fire line. Ahead I see the detour for southbound traffic, which is us.

"I guess it depends on if you like to talk. I'm fine with it."

But I'm not fine with it. "Shouldn't we always have something to say?"

You pause for a moment. "Silence between two people can say a great deal," you offer.

I take your cue. I have this feeling we've climbed down a length of very long rope only to come to an impossibly frayed end. And you're content to just hang here, maybe even let go.

The detour takes us off the highway and over a series of increasingly narrow roads. The land on either side is parched, yellow and flat, not a single green lawn in front of the few houses here and there, all of them squat like half-melted candles. We're following a trailer-pulled car, a dusty-red wagon with orange-centered taillights like jet engines and chrome-trimmed tail fins jutting out like horn-rimmed glasses.

"The back of that car reminds me of my mother," you say, "when she used to wear those awful black bifocals."

"There," I yell. "I was just thinking that. The thing about the glasses."

You don't even have to ask. I can see you understand I'm talking about my clairvoyance. You just shake your head. I look out the window. There are more houses here. We're getting closer to a town. "There's a kid home from school with lice," I say. "His parents have shaved his head and he's been watching soap operas all day. The doorbell rings. It's a woman, a neighbor. She's surprised. 'I've got lice,' the boy says.

"'Tell your dad I'll come back later,' she says. 'Will you be here tomorrow?' The boy shakes his head and goes back to the TV. His dad comes in the room. 'That was Mrs. Ebersol,' the boy says. The father is a bit flustered. 'Dad?' the boy asks. 'Do we use tampons?' '*We* don't.' The father laughs. 'But your mother does.' The boy nods and turns toward the television. 'If we go to the store,' he says over his shoulder, 'I can show you which ones are the most absorbent.'"

"Come on," you finally break in. "You're making that up."

"No." I want to be more adamant, wave my hands or something, but I'm driving.

"You are not psychic."

"Clairvoyant," I say. "How do you explain what I see if I'm not?"

"Your imagination is a flower with an invisible stem," you say.

"I can tell the difference. This stuff I see really happens."

You're silent for miles but finally you feel sorry for me. I want to tell you I know you feel sorry for me, but we'll just start all over again. Then you offer me a consolation. "What brand does the kid recommend?"

We roll into a slim strip of a town. Every restaurant parking lot is full. All this diverted traffic must be a boon. Both of us are hot and I pull into the Airy Queen, the capital *D* and lowercase *a* painted over, changed. There's something about Florida and signs and paint.

Inside, we sit across from each other over our drinks without letting the straws from our lips. Here, too, every logo has been altered to say *Airy Queen*. They're not even trying to be subtle. I know you notice all this, too—the never-changed red seats and scratched white tabletops, the teenage boy mopping the floor in a generic blue uniform, rolls of neck fat curled over his collar. You look around and approve of the minimal remodeling. "It's like a hundred-year-old woman buying a new coat," you say. "Why bother?"

"As long as the sodas are cold." My straw gurgles at the bottom of my already-empty cup and I look up at you. I want to know.

"What's happening?" I ask.

"We've been together a long time. I guess this is the part where we learn to enjoy not having to surprise each other."

Before I can say anything, the kid mopping the floor arrives near our table and swipes the blackish mop near our feet, squeezing it into a bucket of even blacker water. "This is about the busiest day we've had since I've been here," he says. We nod, thinking he's going to continue mopping, but he leans for a moment on his mop handle. "Where you two from?" He's thick and pimply and has a wheezy voice. He wears a gold name tag with no imprint.

"Los Angeles," I say. "Pasadena."

The kid considers this for a moment and smiles. "You all are going to have an earthquake that cracks California right off into the ocean." I know you won't let that pass. I remember once you had an argument with a woman at the bookstore. You insisted that H. G. Wells was scientifically unsound.

"Actually," you tell the kid with the mop, giving me a small kick under the table, "it's the other way around. I'm a seismologist." The kid looks confused, so you say, "We're the people who figure out how strong an earthquake is."

"Seismologist," the kid repeats as if he understands.

"When the big one hits," you continue, "it isn't California that's going to fall into the ocean. We figured out the rest of the continent is kind of supported by the West Coast, like a bearing wall. We figure everything past the Sierra Nevada is going to sink into the Atlantic."

"Really?" the kid asks, but he's looking at me.

"I just sell antique furniture," I say.

He looks at you. "Really?"

"It's fifty-fifty," you say. "Why do you think so many people move to California?"

The kid shakes his head and starts mopping again. He's probably thinking about how much money he has to save to move. You're trying not to laugh and you have that look on your face, the proud one, high eyebrows, pinched smile. It's the same look you had the night we watched the wildfire sunset that you said was like a rainbow. We were on the roof of a parking garage in Pasadena after an early dinner. It was the top floor and we had the only car on that level. You walked me to the corner with this same smile, and we watched the sun go down. We were behind a large exhaust vent and started kissing, all of Old Town spread out below us. "I want to try something," you whispered in my ear. You undid my clothes, stripped me, and turned me toward the city, the yellow streetlights popping on just at the moment, etching new color on the brick buildings. Then you put two of your fingers in my mouth and moved them around slowly. You took them out and suddenly you were doing something new, using them in me, first one, then both, gently sliding in and out, touching a spot inside that felt like small electric shocks each time you made a pass, until in one surprising moment I came. You kissed me on the back of the neck and I braced myself on the ledge with both hands, my legs quivering slightly. "I'll meet you in the car," you said.

The sun is getting low, looking hollow and smoke orange. It cuts a molten swath between the buildings, over the long line of diverted traffic and into the big glass window that separates us from the outside. On the table next to us is a newspaper. One of the headlines says *Aids Wanted.* I look at it long enough to understand it's an article about assisting the elderly. I pick up my cup and pat some ice into my mouth. You don't seem to be thinking anything. If anyone had asked, I'd never have told them that this is how we'd end up, satisfied by silence in a failed ice cream franchise. You stand up, ready to go, but I don't move. "I want to know what's wrong with us. Why aren't we in love anymore?"

Now you look impatient, running your straw in and out of the lid of your cup. This is how you always get if I persist, if I insist on any kind of definition. "Sex does not equal love," you say. "I care for you without having sex." And then you lean in on the table, run a hand through your hair, and look at me hard. "We've had so much sex, we've run up a surplus. It's not going to be like it was."

"Never?"

"Not soon. That part of us is over, at least the amount." You smile and put your hand on mine, which is unusual for you. No public displays of gentle affection. "We just have different ideas about love. I'm starting to think it's as simple as a debt between two people."

Your hand touching mine is surprisingly cold, probably from your cup. You pull it away.

"What do you think we owe each other?" I ask.

"I'd never have gotten the Caltech gig without you," you say. "You pushed me. And maybe I've dragged your flat ass out of a life of predictability. And you've got employees now."

I smile. You smile. "On behalf of the flat-ass clan, I thank you," I say.

"So *that's* love," you say, and like a tractor plowing through a pile of loose hay, you add, "and sometimes love isn't a good enough excuse to stay together."

It's early evening and we're on the road north. Skipping the Magic Kingdom. Did I predict that or just wish it? I didn't ask what you meant back there in Airy Queen because I was afraid. I just gave a noncommittal nod hoping that would pass. The sky to the west is a thin bluish-beige line. No Orlando means no gym and no shower for each of us. We'll be ripe for New Orleans. Since you want to drive the last stretch, I slide down in my seat and close my eyes, thinking about the people onstage getting paid for having sex, the people I know we'll see. I think of Black men with wide shoulders and tight skin slimming down to abs like unseeded garden rows, tight, muscled hips and all of it a slick arrow coming to a point in a big dark penis, and white guys with pink nipples and that kind of creaminess their skin takes on with sex sweat, the dark pubic hair over dicks that never get so long but plump up if girth is your thing, and white women, slender as boned fish but somehow keeping all the curves, asses smooth as sand dunes and silent blonde hair that wants to fall over their eyes, Black women, bigger dunes, a wideness that asserts itself, skin that darkens just right at the joints, and breasts that aren't for amateurs. I think of all of them, the men and women with their sweet spots and those places where fingers and tongues belong. This is what we'll see in New Orleans. This is what's going to remind you how it was for us.

We've stopped. I open my eyes slightly and you're lying back in your seat, eyes staring at the ceiling of the car. It's hot, so hot my back is completely wet. I guess you got tired. I reach over and touch your hand and you look at me. "Can we try?" I ask.

"Sure," you say.

I roll over to kiss you. We're in the dim corner of a rest stop. "Where are we?"

"Somewhere."

I look into your eyes. I look. I do not remember how to kiss you. I tell you this.

"That's okay," you say and you undo your belt and mine. We take off our wet T-shirts and slide our pants to our ankles. These bodies should know each other. I reach for my gym bag but you stop me. "No toys. Let's just use our hands," you say. "We don't want to get too messy."

I'm above you, naked, not wanting to touch you because of the heat, constricted by the space and the pants around my ankles, the steering wheel in my back, not even remembering how to touch you, afraid to do the wrong thing. We start to laugh on some mutual cue and the moment is over.

"What now?" I ask.

"Let's put on our clothes and finish the trip," you say.

I've been standing in front of the same New Orleans crypt for half an hour trying to figure this out. The liquid brown thickness at the bottom of the candle jar is a soup of dead cockroaches. They are fermenting in layers, progressively lightening until the top with its five struggling roaches trying to escape the glass. The jar sits in front of this wall of granite. Above the name is the carved, weathered image of a robed woman, sitting, her hand to her forehead in grief, a cracked planter of water-starved purple vines stretching upward against the stone. Next to it is the cockroach jar, and just above, one readable date, *1899.*

The cockroaches skitter on their hind legs, standing against the glass walls of the jar. I wonder if this is part of a curse or a prayer, a long grudge or unsuppressed hope. It is late afternoon, so hot and humid I'm sweating from just standing. Long shadows shift in intensity as empty thunderclouds pass over the sun. I see you at the front of the cemetery. The car fits perfectly in the entrance space. The walls begin on either side of you, all crypts as well, crumbling red brick between each arched coffin space, stacked three high all the way around. The center is filled with thick rows of gray-stone crypts, some of them with fifteen sealed coffins. Nearly all of them are surrounded by wrought iron and crowned by eroded crosses or decapitated saints. Many façades have crumbled, revealing simple brick and mortar. And there you are in our gray Toyota, the gatekeeper. You honk. It's time to go.

On the outer wall of the cemetery is a flyer with hand-cut phone-number strips. It says *Earn $2,000 a week from your home.* I tear off a number. "Here," I say as I get back in the car, into the shock of air-conditioning. "Quit your job and let's move. Two thousand a week for just sitting at home."

"Thanks," you say, "but I'm still waiting for the right pyramid scheme. Did you get enough?"

You're talking about my insistence that we stop at a cemetery. I want to tell you about the cockroaches, how I want to go back and save them, how I was afraid of some voodoo backlash, a sudden spinal pain, but I just nod and you start the car. When I was a child in Blue Falls, after the first heavy, cold rains that rolled over the Columbia, I'd go out into the street and save earthworms from the puddles, toss them onto lawns or flower beds and give them a second chance. Now I wonder if I was messing with something bigger than I thought. If I screwed up some master plan and I'm paying for it now.

"We can head for the French Quarter," you say, "find a parking space, and look for the place."

"I wish we knew the name."

"We'll find it."

You drive on instinct and it doesn't take us long before we're stuck behind a mule-driven cart with two thick-browed tourists riding in the back. The driver wears a trim straw hat with a black band, the whip in his gravy-brown hands, a slender pole hanging at a not-so-threatening angle to the right.

It feels as if we're driving through slightly enlarged versions of the crypts, close-packed buildings, wrought iron, French windows instead of coffin spaces. But maybe the difference is that everything here is held together somehow by a tenuous coat of newness. The white trim is sharp in the late-afternoon light, and the ironwork of the sagging balconies looks sturdy somehow, thickened by years of paint. I feel suddenly optimistic, as if everything between us is going to be all right.

"Look for the place," you tell me.

"What are we looking for?"

You give me a tight look of frustration. "I'm not sure. Something that says *Sex Show*, I suppose." You make a turn so we're not behind the mule cart anymore but it puts us behind another, this one black as a hearse, a family in the back and the driver pointing at every other building. We drive like this for fifteen minutes until you will a space on the street and a car pulls out from the curb and we slip in.

We walk to Bourbon Street, past a shop with stacked, glazed heads of baby alligators, jaws in mid-snap, past a screened club window with the silhouette of a woman dancing topless, past a completely silver-coated woman wearing a silver toga and holding silver grapes, standing still as a statue for contributions in her silver dish. What makes us stop is a man in a tight black turtleneck. He stands at the door of a bar. "You two sweethearts look hot," he says in a quiet lisp. His toupee is too thick and too dark for his age. He's wearing makeup, foundation. "Free Jell-O shooters for the next hour." We walk on.

Even in the fading daylight it's not getting any cooler. My hair sticks to my forehead. The air is like a drop cloth of invisible steam. It smells like wet concrete and alcohol and urine. It smells sweet. And except for washing down in a rest stop bathroom, neither of us have bathed in two days.

"We should've brought shorts," you say, tapping me on the leg to indicate you're stopping for a beer. The bar stands open to the street, blue neon light spilling onto the sidewalk like pooled water. Just beyond that, a group of Black kids, boys, smash aluminum cans, and attach them to their worn sneakers. One of them is already done. His red cap sits in front of him, already seeded with some change and a dollar bill. He scrapes out a beat, a scratchy tap dance. Sometimes I feel like I'm doing this same thing for you.

You come out with two beers. Across the street, trombone-heavy Dixieland breaks out, and on our side, an electric guitar starts the blues. This seems to be the call. The sidewalks begin to fill with more people. Things are suddenly in gear, and now that I've something to compare myself to, I realize I'm tired.

You tug at my elbow and point. A large sign bordered by flashing light bulbs says *World-Famous Love Acts*. "Do you think that's it?"

"Maybe," I say. We walk over to take a closer look. This is the place. The outside walls are covered with faded photographs of discreetly posed white men and women in sexual positions, nothing we haven't tried. They are on a small stage, the men wearing tight gold lamé bikini shorts, the women the same, with string tops. None of them are in shape and they're smiling, not out of pleasure, but almost like they're winning at a game. One couple is posed in the doggie position. The man's hairy gut rests on the woman's ass as she stares at the camera, bleached-blonde hair falling in front of her half-lidded eyes. Above all of this is a smaller sign that reads *World-Famous Love Acts. The most erotic spot on Earth! Come in and take home what you learn! You'll never be the same!*

"Not as impressive when you see it all in front of you like that," you say, a tilt to your head as you examine the photographs. You sound matter-of-fact, like this is something you expected all along.

"Maybe it's better inside," I say.

You look at me and speak softly. "Be honest, Bit. Would they have *these* pictures on the *outside* if it was any better on the inside?"

A woman in a shiny copper-colored sarong steps out of the doorway with a stack of slim papers in hand, a blare of slow rock following her before it's pinched off by the closing door. "You two oughta come in," she says, winking, allowing us a full view of her bright-green eye shadow. She holds out two of the papers. "A drink on the house."

"Do they have their clothes on the entire time?" you ask her.

The woman smiles. Her red lipstick shines under the flashing lights. "We can't talk about the love acts on the street. But I promise you'll have a wild time." She continues holding out the drink tickets.

You grab my hand and turn to me, eyes wide open, eyebrows high. "What do you think?"

"To be honest," I say, "I'm tired." But what I want to say is that I can't believe you're holding my hand again. I want to say I already know what you're thinking. That you love me. That we don't need this. We should just go off and be by ourselves. That all along we both knew that this wasn't going to be the climax of our road trip You understand the same thing I do, that we're in this for the long haul and this show won't mean anything to us. We know how to have sex and we're going to. It's not over. If I've ever had a truly clairvoyant moment, it's now. I can see what you're thinking. I can see the future. "I feel like we've been on the road a hundred years," I say.

"You're reading my mind," you answer, and you give me an odd look of sympathy. You turn to the woman, letting go of my hand, emptying the space between us. "I'm sorry," you tell her. "It's been a long century and we're exhausted."

settlement

A red pear sat in the middle of a room in a house not yet constructed. The pear was not on a table, as one might suspect, but on the wood floor, which was yet to be installed. Our daughter who had not yet been born walked across the floor that was not there in the house that was not yet constructed. She bit into the pear, which was not ripe and would never be. She began to tear from eyes not yet formed and reached out to us. We did not comfort the daughter not yet born. It wouldn't have been fair because we changed our minds about her.

fuzzling

She ate the cookies.

He knew she ate the cookies but was afraid to confront her.

Her mother was visiting in three days and the apartment was a mess.

They cleaned because it was the one pop-up obsession they were always into.

She walked out of the bathroom and told him she was pregnant.

He said, "Fuck."

She took out the recycling.

He called Dave.

Dave was no help.

She called Dorian.

Dorian used the word "options" too many times.

When she came back to the apartment he asked her why she ate the cookies.

"That's what's on your fucking mind?" She was beside herself.

He was beside himself, but he smiled. "I never want our child to go without cookies."

She touched her lean belly.

The word "hostage" came to mind but instead he offered, "What do you want to do?"

She told him exactly. "I want to get married."

He fuzzled and pulled at his hair.

"To the baby's father," she said. "I'm sorry."

He was relieved, then deeply sad.

It was a difficult pregnancy.

librarians on ice

Engine oil. Not blood.

Theresa turns on the radio and hits the garage-door button. The space moans to life, gray light creeping over the family car that her mother promised would already be moved. It's the same every Saturday morning, even the radio, which launches out of a commercial into electric guitar, music her mother plays because it "reminds her of Daddy." Theresa finds her own station, which is heavy on advertisements for mattresses and, lately, a traveling ice show. The music is a piece she isn't familiar with, piano and saxophone, instruments she can play but chooses not to. "I ran out of notes," she tells anyone who asks. Preparing for the day, she adjusts the light-blue barrettes she's chosen to match her T-shirt, the one with a pair of smiling blueberry kittens. It was a gift for her eleventh birthday and, though it's a bit tight, she wears it to remind herself how little she's grown in the past two years.

Fully lit, the garage reveals a perimeter lined with books three shelves high, some on roll-away carts leaving just enough space for the car. Theresa squeezes through to the end where, outside, the neighborhood hisses with automatic sprinklers, liquid circles wider than the square lawns. Wet sidewalks reflect silhouettes of queen palm trios. *Tarantulas on flagpoles*, she thinks. A perfect day to run away, something she's been thinking about more and more. *I'm not one of these people*, she tells herself, thinking of her parents. In the garage she has a red backpack stuffed with granola bars, water, and a city map, a stash she's maintained for weeks, just in case. She knows the route she would follow, has counted the number of steps it would take to be out of sight. But now, as always, she thinks of her books and the people who need them. Within an hour, there will be joggers and dog walkers and people coming to see Theresa.

"Mom," she yells, turning inside. "The car. I need to open."

Wagon in oleander bushes two blocks away.

Last year it was Franz Liszt with Ozawa conducting. This year it is books, hardcovers, Ayn Rand and Charles Lindbergh. *China on Horseback* and *The Land of Emperors*, Norman Mailer, Virginia Woolf, any book that sounds like knocking on a door when you thump it with a knuckle. What started during the school year as an obsession with scouring thrift stores and yard sales has turned into a garage full of books, those purchased and those given to her; a library of one's own. Now, actually, a library for the neighborhood every Saturday from 8:00 A.M. to 5:00 P.M.

Because it is a normal weekend, Theresa's mother is leaving for Bikram yoga, and afterward she will meet Theresa's father for their weekly counseling session, about which she only hears, "Your dad and I are trying." They have been *trying* for two years with the counseling, lunch afterward, and once-a-week sleepovers at his apartment without Theresa. She has honed a line to explain this, complete with dramatic pause. "My mother and father are separated and dating—each other."

Out of the house with her water bottle and lavender yoga mat, Theresa's mother offers a smile. "Morning, sweets," she says. Theresa thinks of her mother as basically kind but excessively bouncy and a bit obvious about trying to act younger than she is. Her clothes are tight and cut too short at the midriff. Today, her red hair is pulled into a thick, braided ponytail that swooshes back and forth like a hyperactive metronome. Theresa plays a game with it, trying to find even a flash of discernible beat. She pulls at her kitten shirt from the bottom so that it's flat against her body. She wonders if her mother will recognize the old gift, perhaps notice that her daughter will never have a figure like hers. *Not a gene in common*, Theresa thinks.

"Yoga," her mother says as she throws her gym bag into the back seat of the car. "Then counseling with Dad. You know the routine." She slips inside the car, but popping back up briefly, "Hey," she says, "cute shirt. Be nice to Mrs. Peeger."

It would be impossible not to be nice to Mrs. Peeger, Theresa thinks. She is the woman across the street who's watched her ever since they brought her home from China as an infant. Mrs. Peeger would *get* the kitten shirt. She has never forgotten a birthday or Christmas, comes over with pieces of coconut cake and potted orchids she grows in her backyard. Once, she allowed Theresa to wear her daughter's childhood sari to school. In exchange, Theresa does small things, the pinching and twisting things that Mrs. Peeger's arthritic wrists can't handle anymore. A week ago Theresa repaired a decapitated concrete gosling the gardener hit with the mower.

As Theresa's mother pulls out of the driveway a line of morning light drools across the roof. Theresa fixes her face into a stern, narrow-eyed expression and crosses her arms, hoping for the perfect pose to gnaw at her mother if this turns out to be a final memory of her daughter. As usual, though, the car accelerates down the street without another glance from her mother, the rolled yoga mat mocking Theresa from the back window like a favored child headed for ice cream.

Mrs. Peeger, always on cue, steps outside in her denim gardening clothes and tattered straw hat. She waves and calls to Theresa. "If you need anything, sanam, I'll be out back," she says. Her voice is high and informally melodic. "See you at lunchtime." *If it weren't for Mrs. Peeger*, Theresa thinks, *I could disappear*. Just walk off. Maybe to Chinatown. Blend in. This is something on her mind a little more every day. She wonders if her parents considered even for a second that their daughter would look nothing like them. *Adopted.* She knows it's the first thing people think when they see the three of them together, which lately, isn't that often.

A green van. No license plate.

"I haven't read this since I was a boy," Mr. Halvo says, handing Theresa *The Red Badge of Courage.* He's a regular, returns his books promptly. Theresa judges by his white hands and arms with their random plinks of gray hair that he's rarely in the sun. His face is the same, except pinkish in the cheeks and nose.

"So how are you?" he asks as she logs his selection.

Theresa doesn't look up. "Adequate," she says. It's her new word to replace "fine." This term seems less ambiguous, more honest. Adequate means nothing in excess. All needs are being met at least at a minimal level.

"Well," Mr. Halvo says, caught off guard, "could be worse. Listen, I guess you've never heard of Audie Murphy?"

This Theresa likes. Questions suggesting strange information. She writes the name and breaks it down. *A. Murphy—Murphy, Audy—Oddy.* She looks around at the garage with its rows of bookshelves rolled into place. Not an author and definitely not anyone she's ever checked a book out to. "Does she live in this neighborhood?"

Mr. Halvo laughs and takes a pen out of his shirt pocket, writing the correct spelling above Theresa's note. His print is unsteady, jagged, but readable. "Audie," Mr. Halvo says, sounding pleased he knows something Theresa doesn't. "*He* was a war hero. Movie star too." He points to the book he's about to take home. "Made a great one out of this."

"I'll look it up." Although she is not fond of chitchat, Theresa is relieved that Mr. Halvo is the first person to drop by and that he's in no hurry to leave. Last Saturday her mother allowed a news crew to do a segment on Theresa's summer library.

"Why are they here?" Theresa asked.

"It's a surprise for you, sweets," her mother said. "Your father will be here too."

Theresa immediately forecast the consequences and she was right. All week people have been driving through the neighborhood looking for the house where "the world's youngest librarian" lives. Someone even left a box of used romance novels on the driveway, which Theresa promptly threw into the recycling bin. Except for one called *The Hindi Hero*, which she and Mrs. Peeger had a good laugh over.

This morning, Theresa is relieved to be talking about not much with Mr. Halvo without a stranger in sight. She'd watched the news feature about her book lending with her mother, horrified at the forced shot of her and her parents thumbing through a fat copy of *Gone with the Wind*. At the end of the newscast, the anchorwoman said, "That little girl must have amazing parents." *Adequate*, Theresa thought.

Across the street, Mrs. Peeger's hat and dark eyes poke above her fence as she waves with a glove full of clippings. "Namaskar!" she calls.

Theresa returns the greeting as she delivers Mr. Halvo's selection into his pale, spongy hands. "Something new this week," she says. "I'm letting everyone keep whatever they check out. But don't go telling. I only want people to keep the books they want, not the ones they might want."

Mr. Halvo offers a look of saddened surprise. "Then why write everything down?"

This question strikes Theresa as odd. "Consistency."

"So you're closing down?"

"More like fading away." Theresa walks Mr. Halvo to the lip of the garage. "When people get too used to a thing, it's not special anymore."

Mr. Halvo's face flushes. He looks hurt, abandoned. "It'll be a shame," he says quietly, almost to himself. "The highlight of my week is these little visits with you."

Final entries: Anne of Green Gables, Tales of a Fourth Grade Nothing, Are You There God? It's Me, Margaret.

By 11:00 Theresa has given away fifty-three books, hardly a dent in the shelves. The multicolored spines surrounding her look like some elaborate musical keyboard. She looks for patterns in the colors but instead finds probability. Green and blue spines are the most likely to sit side by side. Those in her China section are all red or black. She'd brought these out from her personal collection. There were a few months when she read everything she could about the country because if she ever found her biological parents she thought she should know about the place they lived. But then she came across a number, one billion. Once a day for a week she wrote it in her journal just to see if familiarity would make it less impossible. *1,000,000,000. 1,000,000,000. 1,000,000,000. 1,000,000,000. 1,000,000,000. 1,000,000,000. 1,000,000,000.* It would take her, she calculated, 31 years, 259 days, 5 hours, 33 minutes, and 20 seconds to count that high. How could she ever find her biological parents in all that humanity? It wasn't like the blonde woman on television who flew to Oklahoma and met her biological mother at the airport. Tears and flowers and television cameras.

Theresa is left with the one thing her mother will say about her adoption, the phrase she is supposed to hold on to like a precious gift made to open anytime she needs reassurance that she is special and chosen. It was late at night, dark, when her mother placed her hands on Theresa's cheeks and spoke. "We took one look at you and said, 'Yes, her.'"

Now, the light beyond the lip of the garage has brightened to a hazy white, the middle part of the day when very few people visit Theresa's library. She stands just out of the sun holding *To Kill a Mockingbird*, which someone pulled off the shelf and didn't replace. The only person on the street is Phillip Brauer who's been riding his new bike around the neighborhood all day. Theresa has never been one for crushes. She finds boys her age to be distracted and clumsy. But Phillip is smart and not her age, fifteen, and sure, a bit showoffy, but with good reason.

For the millionth time Phillip rides by standing on his pedals, jeans sagging below his waist, newly broad shoulders triangulating his torso. His black hair is different than Theresa's, wavy and out of control. This time he makes a sharp turn and rides toward her. What feels like a lit match flares in her chest. "Hey, Treece," he says, his front tire halting a few inches from her. "Hear you're giving away your books."

"Not exactly." But she wants to say, *Yes, Phillip, come in and take all you want.* She wants him to ask her to ride on the handlebars of his bike like she's seen Marrissa Stallers do. At the same time she rushes with hope, Theresa is acutely aware of her smallness.

Philip begins a series of figure eights in the driveway. "I finished it," he says, without looking at Theresa.

She knows exactly what he means. Three weeks ago *Ulysses* was the first book he went to, not because he had any interest in James Joyce, but because it was the fattest book on the shelves. She'd made a cover for the tattered volume out of a grocery bag and written the title in thick black ink on the spine. "What's it about?" Theresa asks.

Phillip drops his feet to the concrete, stopping the bike in mid-curve. Behind him, a blonde woman approaches with four books from last week, Mrs. Corson. Theresa returns to the small, wobbly desk where she keeps her records, each title with its own page. She notices how Phillip waits, almost statue-like but irritated, as Mrs. Corson declines the offer to keep the books, though she does move back to the shelves.

"*Ulysses*," Phillip begins with an unsteady and teacherly voice, "is about this guy Leopold and his family. And Dublin." He pauses, showing in his expression the enormity of summary before him. "It's being young, and getting old, and going crazy with a lot of words in between."

Theresa laughs. "Are you going to keep it?"

"If that's cool, yeah."

It's a word she hates, "cool," so overused, not even adequate, but somehow, on Phillip, it feels authentic. "It's cool," she says, and it comes out easier than she ever imagined.

"Thanks, Treece," he says. "We'll have to go riding sometime like we did when I was a kid." He points to Mrs. Corson and winks. "But seems like I can't ever get you alone."

It is not lost on Theresa that the wink means she isn't included in his leap toward maturity. She knows that as far as Phillip is concerned she is still the little girl with the purple bike. Normally this would be a moment where she would burrow down and dwell but Mrs. Corson steps up with *From Crossbow to H-Bomb.*

"You're busy," Phillip says. "Catch you later. Thanks for the book."

Disappointed, Theresa begins writing down Mrs. Corson's selection to satisfy Phillip's observation. "Cool," she says to Phillip, only this time it comes unplanned, something casual from inside her that she recognizes immediately as the edge of some undiscovered territory. She looks up to see if Phillip heard it in her voice, but he is already off the driveway, legs pumping, narrow back and wide shoulders slanted forward and away.

Theresa takes a breath and explains again to Mrs. Corson that she should keep the book. The summer library is winding down.

Mrs. Corson clutches the history of weaponry, her long maroon nails raking the cover. "What a shame," she says, shaking her head. "You're quite a little prodigy."

"Not really," Theresa says, "merely precocious."

No witnesses.

A little after one there are five people in the garage including Mrs. Peeger who delivered a bowl of curried rice with cubed chicken, most of which sits in front of Theresa as a yellow aftermath. She stares into the dish, visually connecting the grains into constellations: Monoceros, Draco, Canis Major. But then she stops because everything is there between poultry moons. This galaxy and all the known universe collapsed into her bowl. Everything condensed and knowable and at the mercy of a god who's quickly losing interest.

"Sanam," Mrs. Peeger says, still in her denim garden outfit. "I must get back to my orchids. Are you alright for a while?

"Yes, thank you," Theresa says. She has never known her first name. Mrs. Peeger looks at her with mock disappointment and Theresa corrects her error with a sheepish grin. "Dhanya-waadh."

As Mrs. Peeger steps across the street Anna Marks presents Theresa with her selection. "I'd like to check out *Horton Hears a Who!*" she says. "And these." She sets down six other books. "For my sister." Theresa knows better and looks at Anna who is seventeen but still wearing her blonde hair in two ponytails that she eagerly admits she highlights with lemon juice and plenty of sun. Theresa imagines Anna reclined at the beach, bathed in light and armed with citrus and Seuss.

But, Theresa thinks, *I didn't open the library* not *to check out books.* She wonders how she might have turned out if Anna's parents had adopted her. Would Anna's personality be her fate? And what does lemon juice do to Chinese hair?

"Yeah," Anna says as if replying to a question that hasn't been asked. "My mom told me to tell you that Day has asthma again."

Eight-year-old Day Keese lives two blocks over in the white house with a concrete yard that her father washes down every morning before he drives Day to school where she is loaded down with inhalers and tissues and hand sanitizers. She stays healthy all week, but when the weekend comes she falls into another asthma attack. Theresa is beginning to believe this is all somehow induced. No matter what, her parents will not allow her to leave the yard, and so, on the weekends, she is inside and in bed. Even when Theresa delivers books, she never sees Day. Just hands them to Mrs. Keese who wipes them down with a white cloth.

Theresa thinks about what's left that she might bring Day. The first time her parents rejected the book on Greek mythology. "This isn't age appropriate," Mrs. Keese said, the book handed back between pinched fingers. Today, because this will be the last time she delivers, Theresa decides to load her wagon with a few basics: *Anne of Green Gables*, *Tales of a Fourth Grade Nothing*, *Are You There God? It's Me, Margaret.* At the same time, she thinks of another book for Phillip.

Anna huffs, irritated at the wait.

"Tell your mother the final thing I'll do today is bring Day some books."

Last seen in a blue T-shirt with blue kittens. Possibly carrying a red backpack.

Theresa is rereading the titles she's given away today when the phone rings. She looks at the brown unit on the wall with its cord that hangs, python-like, to the concrete floor. Her father stretched it out on weekends when he inspected the paint on his blue Mustang for scratches and nicks and road tar. Penlight and magnifying glass in hand, phone secured between ear and shoulder, no flaw was too small for concern as he spoke to men Theresa never met, repetitive men apparently, who never got tired of discussing things like oil viscosity, carburetors, and rubbing compounds. Things, Theresa wanted to point out, her father had no particular expertise in.

She recalls an evening before her father moved out when he was polishing the car, the garage dizzying with lemony fumes. She'd come out for his company, though now she wonders why she was that desperate. "Dad," she said, "what do you know about China?"

He stood up straight and sighed, a sound that had become his frequent first response. "We were only there for a few days. I remember lots of bikes."

"Oh," Theresa said, bailing out. "Bikes are cool."

"We'll talk about it later, sweets," her father said. "Think about what kind you want."

It's her father on the phone now, as she expected, because he always calls on Saturdays after couple's therapy. "Hi, sweets," he says with a forced brightness. "Mom and I just finished up lunch. She'll be home in an hour or so."

Theresa knows the script. The "or so" part means at least two. "Great," she says.

"So what's up?"

"The same." She sits down at her desk and turns to fresh pages in her checkout log where she freehands straight lines down the ruled paper, challenging herself toward a perfect grid. On the other end of the line she hears her father tapping on something.

"Listen, sweets," he says. "Next week I want to take you to the ice show."

"Oh."

"And Mom too. The three of us. Won't that be cool?" His tone is more matter-of-fact than plaintive, as if he's reading from a prescription bottle. Take one family weekly as needed. Nonrefillable. "They have all your favorite characters."

Has he called the wrong daughter? Theresa wonders. Not even in an alternate universe would she be interested in anything even resembling an ice show. And favorite characters? Years ago when he scooped her up in that Chinese orphanage is this what he projected? That someday he'd take her to a darkened sports arena with a frozen core and call that fatherhood?

As he explains what a wonderful evening they will have, Theresa finds herself drawing figure eights across her finished grid. *My favorite characters?* she repeats in her mind, smiling. She thinks of one, but not from television or movies, imagines a white spotlight moving across a black field, Boo Radley on skates, Scout lifted above him in her ham costume, a drunken Mr. Ewell chasing them both. All of it choreographed to Liszt's *Totentanz*, his danse macabre. She imagines the opening chords, the low notes pounding from the piano, Seiji Ozawa conducting the orchestra at arena's edge, he in all white with trademark mop of silvering black hair.

"So what do you think, sweets?" her father says.

"Great," Theresa says. But she's thinking, *Needs a finale*, a swift, interceding chorus line on blades, sensibly dressed men and women carrying stacks and stacks of glittering books. "Allegro animato," the final two minutes of dark descent born from the keys of a black piano, vortex of skaters swallowing Mr. Ewell with text, the mass of them whirling him away, disappearing behind the large black drapes where true resolution will do its dirty work.

"Me, you, Mom, and all those big fuzzy guys skating around. What could possibly be better?"

Amused by her own production, Theresa replies with the one thing she's certain of. "Librarians on Ice!"

"What?" her father asks. "Oh, right, your little project. I guess you have to go." It's clear he is seizing the opportunity to conclude, and Theresa doesn't mind because she is thinking she will not attend an ice show with this stranger who is checking off a box on some responsible-father list. He might have said concert or gallery instead. She thinks of how often he is one or two words short of understanding. She feels accumulation, critical mass, and knows she cannot be here when her mother gets home.

After she hangs up the phone, Theresa returns to the page filled with her doodles. On it she cannot find Boo or Scout, much less see Mr. Ewell swamped by books. But in the looping congestion of scrawls disrupting the grid, she hears Liszt again, reads each curve as a musical note. She holds up the ledger, the lead from her pencil refracting light, every mark permanent as a skate line on rink ice. *It is possible*, she thinks, *to erase your tracks.*

Finnegans Wake *left in the mailbox of Phillip Brauer.*

The garage door lowers slowly like an eye giving in to sleep. Theresa stands before it as if she's just commanded a giant to slumber. Staying a wagon loaded with the red backpack and her deliveries, she watches her shelves of books darken and disappear beyond the beige door, sealing the contents with an emphatic thump. In her other hand, Theresa holds the remote control, and for a moment considers reopening the door. She has never closed the library this early and worries about someone who might have a specific book in mind. But the street is largely empty on both sides. Down the block, Mr. and Mrs. Palmer are washing their yellow lab, Dolbey, in the front yard, and a green van sits at the intersection while its driver smokes a cigarette.

Mrs. Peeger calls at Theresa from her front door. "Closing up so early?"

"Day Keese again," Theresa says, knowing she need not say more. She waves and turns back toward the house. Mrs. Peeger has given her the first real pangs of reconsideration. She will deliver the books, she tells herself, and after that, she'll see. *Maybe this isn't the day.* She looks at the backpack knowing that its contents won't get her far.

Age thirteen. Chinese ancestry. Possible runaway. Adoptive parents.

The husband and wife have crossed the border between remorse and regret. They remain in darkness facing the garage where they have been sitting in the car without speaking. It's been nearly seven months, but tonight at dinner they heard a child's voice so close to Theresa's they both turned to look. The girl was about their daughter's age, but nothing like her at all. This girl was round and wearing a denim jumper and she wasn't Chinese.

The wife turns from the garage toward her husband. His features are deeply shadowed but the man she loves is there. Beyond him, the dark yard is bruised at the edges by greenish light. "This is ridiculous," she says. "It wasn't our fault. The therapist said so."

Looking at the upholstered ceiling of the car, the husband pushes the remote, the garage door sounding deep and constant like a disturbed hive. Fully opened, it snares the couple in yellow light, stares at them. It is a wide and unblinking eye. At the back are the husband's few remaining moving boxes. Each side of the garage is lined with white sheets draped over shelves of books mountainous as gurneys in a hospital morgue. "Maybe it's time we did something with those," he says.

The wife is reluctant. "If she comes home, she'll be upset with us. And besides, we can't just trash them."

"Of course not," he allows, but he wants to say that after this many months the odds of their daughter turning up are minuscule.

"She'd want people to have them."

"I agree," he says. "I'll call a used bookstore tomorrow. See what they're worth."

As her husband talks about selling the books, the wife looks into the space waiting to receive their car. It makes her feel ill. On the concrete floor is a narrow pile of kitty litter to soak up leaking oil. When the police came, it was swept away and tested. They found engine oil. Not blood.

"I keep thinking about how none of this would have happened if we hadn't adopted her."

"Don't be silly," the husband says. The light from the garage shows his wife's eyes on the verge of tears but he knows neither of them is anywhere near crying.

"Why did we insist on a baby?"

The husband is silent. This is the one subject their therapist seldom got them to discuss. They wanted a family, certainly. But then the question again became why. And for that, their answer, when they had one, changed, pitched, each a structure built on shifting sand.

"I remember our first day home," his wife continues. "She was so small."

"With all that black hair. And crying."

The wife recalls her husband's arm around her waist the first time they watched Theresa sleeping in her crib. "We were just so relieved when she fell asleep. Unprepared from the start."

"We weren't that bad."

"We were," the wife says, placing a hand on her husband's neck. "Our first bit of family bliss was about her silence. You held me and said, 'What could possibly be better?'"

The husband is startled, recalling his last conversation with Theresa. "I know the answer to that question now," he says. "Librarians on Ice."

"What's that supposed to mean?"

The husband releases a lungful of air. "I wish I'd asked," he says.

Frustrated, the wife starts the car and pulls into the garage. "What good's an answer without meaning?" On either side of them Theresa's books are shrouded beneath white sheets.

In front of the car, the husband's stacked moving boxes read *kitchen*, *bathroom*, *laundry*, and *entertainment*. It occurs to him that there wasn't a single book in any of his boxes.

Neither the husband nor wife makes a move to exit the car. Taking a deep breath, she speaks. "Didn't you think it would make a bigger difference? I mean, the first month was hard. But now?"

The husband considers the tattered fliers posted all over town, that initial door-to-door canvassing and the first two weeks when local newscasts showed Theresa's photo every day. And for both of them, there were in fact sleepless weeks of worry, spontaneous wincing at thoughts of what the person who abducted their daughter might have done to her. They could never believe she would run away. In those first weeks every phone ring was renewed loss, exhaustion throwing their limbs into spontaneous cramps and shaking.

"How long," the husband asks, "is long enough?"

"Parents shouldn't have to ask that question." The wife reaches out and holds her husband's hand, though they continue to look forward. "Sometimes," she says quietly, "I think if she was ours, I mean not adopted, that somehow we'd still be wrecks."

The husband looks at his wife, who is still young and beautiful to him. Despite their problems she is the woman he wants a family with. But the truth is, Theresa was part of their difficulties, and if they can't say goodbye to her soon, there may be no second chance for happiness. He is thinking these things and at the same time knows he can never say them. He wonders, in the history of human mourning what percentage is performance?

Minutes pass and the husband and wife continue to hold hands in silence. Though they do not say it to each other, neither wants to squeeze by Theresa's bookshelves with their odd volumes that poke from the sheets like grasping hands. Instead, the couple waits for the light on the garage-door opener to turn itself off. In darkness, Theresa's library will disappear and maybe one of them will find the strength to say what they are both thinking, that their daughter is gone and it is beginning to feel normal. Theresa's disappearance was a shock, but they are coming to understand the trajectory of loss. It is birthed whole and then contracts.

In the seconds after darkness begins its snaps and sutures, the husband and wife arrive at something foreign, something close to unity. Without light it is easy for them to imagine that their long-ago journey to a pillbox orphanage in Shaanxi never really happened. Now, they look in each other's direction, knowing there is nothing to see, creating each other from memory. It's as if they have emerged from an experiment as part of the control group, the pair of them stronger, if unhealed, and still candidates for the cure. Tonight they are a husband and wife holding hands in the dark, thinking it was placebo all along and wondering if they can ever again say, *Yes, her.*

the fish is gone. but the cake is here.

The old dude calls from across the covered patio. "It's the Alps. You are here for trout!" His Slovene accent dominates a cool breeze. He's unshaven, but smiling and bright-eyed behind glasses with thick black frames, entirely clad in even blacker leather motorcycle garb, a helmet in the seat across from him as if it's a dining companion. In one hand he holds a slender green paperback book, which he shakes at us in a way that's teacherly and menacing at once. Beyond him the pine-laced mountain pass leads to a distant canvas of elevation. "Trout," he says again. Chaun and I have been torturing the waitress for a description of everything on the menu. I'm certain I'm getting the three-meat plate. A safe choice. Plus, we are hungry and way off our intended route, and not on purpose. Chaun's fault. It seems appropriate that this place is called Brunarica Slap, because that's what I want to do to him. In two weeks I'm out of a job with no prospects but Chaun insisted on this trip together anyway. Because, we are one after all, Chaun and Gabe. "ChaunGabe," as our friends call us. It could be my passport, or the innkeeper who greets us individually by our first names, but something about Slovenia has reminded me that I like hearing my name apart from Chaun's.

But, here we are, sitting side by side at a table covered by a red-and-white-checkered cloth, the restaurant's only customers besides the old dude obsessed with our order. "The trout," Chaun asks the waitress, "is it whole?" The old dude chuckles as the waitress nods. "I'd like it headless," Chaun continues. More chuckling.

"I'm sorry," the waitress says earnestly, clearly having addressed this question from tourists countless times. "We cannot do this." She stands robust and upright in a white short-sleeved blouse and a red apron tight around her waist. Chaun and I wait for an explanation, but none comes. Instead, she stares firmly at her pad, strong fingers keeping a pencil at the ready for a revised order. "Your decision?" she asks without looking up. I'm less bothered by the abruptness than her collective address, as if there were one decision to be made between the two of us.

More chuckling from our one-man audience who holds up two fingers and rattles off something in Slovene. Our waitress inspects us, then replies over her shoulder. Neither Chaun nor I speak the language, but when the man's tone becomes insistent, if not loud, and she shrugs her shoulders, leaving our table, I know what's happened. We're having trout.

"Did that just . . .," Chaun begins, but he's cut off by the old dude who approaches us with a beer and the helmet that holds his book.

"The three-meat is good," the old dude says, plopping himself down across from us, "but I've ordered for you the trout." We begin to object, but the man raises a thick-fingered hand and smiles broadly, small gaps between each tooth. "I know. How dare I impose," he continues, puffing up his chest as if to mock his own bravado. "But it is what they are known for. My wife would slap my head for this. But as you see, she's not here."

There is something disarming in his honesty, and anyway, lost or not, it's a perfect day to sit in this covered patio surrounded by trees, a golden-oak ceiling gleaming above as if it were the sun itself, though not the south Florida sun I'd have preferred. Chaun and I look at each other, exchanging silent permission to accept this adventure however it turns out. We've come to Slovenia for our tenth anniversary, five married. Chaun is a photographer and political poet, part of a loose group of Chicago writers called Queer Riot. So, of course we've come to the land of the poets. I had suggested the Florida Keys, but here we are. In any case, this trip is a prelude to another, more important one. In weeks, Chaun will visit his aging parents in Calgary. They know nothing about his poetry nor about me, which is why they are making one more try at matchmaking. Apparently the unsuspecting woman is twenty-seven and from a wealthy Hong Kong family just like Chaun's parents were. I've insisted, at last, that at thirty-nine years old, it's time he tell them he's gay and has a husband. He's insisted that if he does, it will leave them childless and him without parents. "You have me," I said. He didn't reply but the silence sounded like, "You're not enough." I'm almost okay with that.

"I'll put some lettuce over the eyes or something," Chaun says about the trout. "I went through an entire childhood staring at fish heads and that was enough."

"Yes, yes," the man says, clapping his hands together. "You are Chinese. Of course!"

"Chinese American," Chaun says.

The man laughs. "I've been to America many times. I know about your obsession with hyphens. I am Slovene. And you?" He looks me up and down. "I'm guessing you are about five or six hyphens. Typical white American. Yes?"

"He's got you pegged," Chaun laughs.

If typical is going-gray scruff and a little extra weight, I am indeed pegged. I love Chaun, though he insists that I say this too often to him and declare it to too many people. Maybe I do this to remind myself that at first he was the "hot Asian guy" at the gym my friends got tired of hearing about. I timed my workouts to what I figured were his. I'd enter the floor and look for his amazing shock of black hair and the crisply lined poison ivy tattoo trailing down from the back of his neck and into his tank top. I confessed to him on our fifth date that no matter where I was in my workout, if he finished and hit the showers, I was shortly behind. He rolled his eyes. "That's hardly news," he said. Occasionally he reminds me that was our fourth date, not the fifth, because the first time, he was standing at his car door in the gym parking lot, waiting for me. His hair was still damp, a black swoosh over one eye. We gave each other a chin-led 'sup as I passed, and then I looked back and it was on. He lived just two blocks away. Afterward, we exchanged numbers in case, well, definitely not to get coffee. Turns out you can hook up *and* get coffee.

"Matic," the man says, introducing himself. "I stop here every time I tour. Even with my wife."

My husband raises a finger. "Chaun, and Mr. Three-Meat here is Gabe." Then he looks around. "Where is she? Your wife."

Matic shrugs, and his eyes widen at the sight of our water glasses. "Sparkling? You must have *beer* with trout. *This* trout anyway." He calls inside and gets a response from the waitress.

"Dark or light?" he asks us.

"We're cool," I say, giving Chaun an accusatory glance.

"Bah." Matic isn't having it and once again calls to the kitchen. "You will have half dark, half light." He holds up his near-empty glass. "I drink this in such good weather."

Chaun's not letting go. "You're traveling with your wife and you don't know where she is?"

"Yes! Right. But I see my error. I believe when I say 'with,' Americans hear 'together.' I mean 'at the same time,' or . . .," he searches, ". . . 'simultaneous'? Yes. 'Simultaneous.'" He explains that he and his wife plan vacations and tours in proximity, but not necessarily with the same itinerary. Today she has ridden her motorcycle to Lake Bled.

"We're thinking about hitting that in a couple of days," I say. It's an alpine lake, a famously brilliant-green inset gem guarded by a medieval castle. Practically every brochure and website for Slovenia includes its image.

Chaun raises an eyebrow. "I don't remember that conversation."

"Right. *I* was thinking about it."

Matic sticks his tongue out. "Too many tourists, Gabe. The two of you, look at this." He gestures around us, though for a second I fall behind because he's said my name. "Today I met you. You met me. We are having the right food. At Bled they pretend for the tourists. Here I ask the woman to bring you trout and she does because it's the right thing. You will tell your friends at home about this day. We sit in the cathedral of life." He points behind us at a picture bolted to the sloped ceiling. "And there is our Madonna." She's a black-booted woman astride a vintage motorcycle. And clad in a leather bikini top, long black gloves and a leather biker cap.

Brando, double D.

Chaun laughs. Lake Bled has been dismissed. "Don't ever open a restaurant in Boystown," he says to Matic, who clearly doesn't get the reference. "It's a gay neighborhood in Chicago. We're used to getting what we want."

"You two?" Matic is suddenly aware of the rings on our fingers, and I observe that he isn't wearing one. He nods his head and points to Chaun. "*You*, I understand. Asian men can be inclined this way, and you are very groomed. But this one . . . Gabe, you could lift my motorcycle."

Chaun's eyes are glazed in shock as he quickly stands. If Matic didn't notice us when we came in, I know he will be surprised by Chaun's height. It's all in his legs. "Did you fucking just say that?" Chaun says. I put my hand on his knee to calm him. He's heard some form of this insult for most of his adult life. When he was younger he told me that dating was a mess because every guy that asked him assumed he was a bottom. I did too, though I've never told him. "I'm going for a smoke," Chaun says. Maybe because his parents are on his mind, he's saving all his energy for that conflict, because it's clear he isn't taking Matic on. "Call me when our food comes out."

Matic places both hands flat on the table as Chaun walks away. "It was this Asian-gay comment, wasn't it? I can apologize. I meant nothing by it."

I should be angry for Chaun, but I've never really worried about these assumptions and stereotypes. Fem. or masc. Top or bottom. Sub or Dom. Rice queen. Snow queen. Whatever.

I'm not political that way, but it's what Chaun writes about. He's been challenged far more often on these fronts than I. He says my dispassion comes from white privilege and I suppose he's right. "Matic, that's a sore spot for sure," I muster. "Maybe you should go back to your table before my husband comes back." As I say this, the waitress brings out three beers, but Matic points to his original table where she delivers his glass.

"We were having such a nice time."

My empathies in the moment are misplaced, I know it, but

Matic sounds genuinely sorry, and I find myself unexpectedly happy with the scenario. One of us has bolted without the other.

"It's a sensitive subject," I tell Matic.

"Of course," Matic says, gathering his helmet and standing. "In my twenties I was with a man, Albin, for almost two years." His expression tightens as if calling the memory of this former lover forward in his mind. "He wanted me to come out, as you say. It was very difficult. I wasn't gay. I only loved *him*." Matic walks toward his table, but turns before he makes it all the way. "The waitress says the trout is taking a little longer because they had to bring it up." He points over the railing, and then it's as if I've just walked in, there's an old dude at the rear of the patio in black-leather motorcycle gear staring into a beer and sitting across from his bicycle helmet. I want to give Chaun the all clear, but his posture across the narrow parking lot suggests that I give him a minute. He's leaning on the front of our rental, arms crossed, cigarette smoke gliding upward past his face. If I wasn't already married to him, I'd ask that man out. I feel like an idiot sitting alone in the middle of the patio, so I walk with my beer to the railing. The half-light, half-dark beer is pretty good. There's a mountain stream just behind the restaurant and, on the hillside, the terraced trout farm comprised of three rectangular ponds. Above these, six sheep with clotted wool sit beneath the shade of a tree. They are still enough to be statues.

The waitress sweeps behind me and places what looks like a slice of marble rye in front of Matic just as his phone rings. He speaks in Slovene for a few seconds, and then, clearly for my benefit, says loudly, "No, no. The fish is gone. But the cake is here. How is Lake Bled?" Beyond him is that postcard view of pine forest and towering Alpine mountains pinned against a clear blue sky. I should be awed, but all I can think is *What the hell am I doing here?* I could be on the beach in Key West with a rum and Coke getting a little jealous at all the men and women ogling my shirtless husband, knowing they are thinking, *What's he doing with* him*?* There are moments when I catch our reflection side by side and wonder the same thing.

That first day when we hooked up after the gym, showered, Chaun surprised me as we exchanged numbers. "I'm going to check out this show before it closes. Go with?" He handed me a one sheet from the Art Institute of Chicago advertising an exhibit on illustrated books of poetry. I didn't know anything about poetry and wasn't into art, but I'd just been fucked by the hottest guy of my life, a guy I'd obsessed over for months, and he was asking me out.

"Cool," I said, looking at the nasty gym clothes I'd put back on. "But . . ."

"It's not prom."

"There won't be dancing?"

Chaun smiled. "Hold on a second," he said, trotting off to the bedroom. When he came back he was wearing his gym clothes as well. He stood in the door frame, cocked his head, and flung out his arm. "I doubt Miró cares what we wear." I laughed at the gesture and wracked my brain trying to think who the hell Miró was. My education was on.

Ten years later . . . our trout arrives. Chaun has been watching because he returns just as the waitress leaves our table. "Can you believe he said that?" He's still livid but he keeps his voice down as he sits across from me.

"He feels bad. He had a boyfriend once . . . a lover, anyway."

Chaun offers a surprised expression but is not ready to relent. "Let's just eat." The plates in front of us are indeed whole trout, fried golden, head to tail. Strangely, Matic ordered french fries for Chaun and a kind of fish salad for me. After the first bite of trout Chaun and I look at each other. The flavor is so intense and savory that I see in Chaun's eyes it might have the power, if only for seconds, to wipe away homophobia and racism all at once.

"Okay," he says. "I'll give him props for this." Matic is watching, and I nod in appreciation. He gestures with his beer not so much in reply as in directing me to drink mine along with the fish. I comply, and if it's possible, the trout bursts with even more flavor.

"I think you should give our friend a chance to apologize."

"For saying out loud the things he actually thinks?"

"For saying out loud what he assumed *everyone* thinks." I stab my fork into one of Chaun's fries and slowly bring it to my mouth. "He *did* have a boyfriend," I quietly repeat before filling my mouth.

"Hard to believe," Chaun whispers.

"That's what he says."

"And Asian I suppose?" Chaun looks past me. Matic is texting, glasses propped on his forehead. "He's married."

"*We're* married."

"Not to women."

Chaun startles me, not even allowing a beat. "Hey, man," he calls. "That was bullshit what you said, but we're on vacation and I'm not going to spoil it by holding a grudge."

Matic smiles. "You're practically quoting our poet Tomaž Šalamun. He used to tell me I was full of shit all the time. And my wife. She says this too. You are in good company." He raises his nearly empty glass and speaks in Slovene. "This is a saying that means something like 'Even a fool can learn from his mistakes.' I'm sorry for my offense."

"Okay," Chaun says. "And for the record, there wouldn't be so many people in China if the men were 'inclined that way.'" It almost jumps out of my mouth, almost, but I rein it in. I want to call Chaun out for insinuating that gay men don't procreate but an apology has been offered and accepted, the fish is good, the beer is good, so I let it go. And anyway, Chaun isn't done. "You mentioned Šalamun. I love his work. You knew him?"

"Tomaž? Of course. We set this world right many evenings."

I have no idea who these two are talking about, but I hear in Chaun's voice that the fire is out, though I've known him long enough he may be keeping an ember in storage. "*Poker.* I loved that book."

Matic laughs and he's back at the table next to us in a flash managing at the same time to call out for another beer. "That was young Šalamun! Americans always mention this book. It's perhaps a bit loose for my taste. But the energy is there." The waitress sets a beer in front of each of us even though Chaun and I are barely halfway through our first. “I guess you are a poet then,” Matic says. “Only a poet would know that book. And academics.”

“I’d like to think I’m a poet,” Chaun says. “I’ve published. But I pay the bills as a photographer.”

Matic doesn’t ask, but I offer anyway that I’m an executive director of a homeless-shelter nonprofit. I like to tell people this because it makes me sound like I’m a better person than I am. After all, I draw a salary and it isn’t my life’s work. It’s work. Chaun knows this about me now, but early on I wasn’t quite so forthcoming. There was a day when we planned to go to the dog park on Lake Michigan but I needed to stop by one of my shelters in Lincoln Park first. “Even on Saturdays?” Chaun asked. “Especially on Saturdays,” I replied. He was impressed with my dedication to the homeless. I wasn’t noble, and I didn’t mention staff had been warned about being a little substance groggy on weekend mornings. Then again, he failed to mention in those first few months that he was having sex with four other guys. I suppose I won.

Chaun is well into his trout as Matic holds forth on Slovene poetry. He has a favorite, Kosovel somebody, and he mentions the godfather of poetry in this country, Prešeren. He takes a gulp of beer and looks to the ceiling. “And you must very much read Iztok Osojnik. This one is still alive. I think in Ljubljana.” This is our anchor city while we’re on this trip, which is why the mention of Prešeren comes as no surprise to me. There’s a massive statue of him looming over the main square. In fact, we have seen no statues of generals or political leaders. Only poets.

Chaun types this information into his phone, asking for spelling. These two are getting along famously now. "You know a lot about poetry," I say.

"Of course. I'm Slovene."

"And your wife?"

"Maja? Does she know poetry? Yes, but this is a complicated question because she prefers women poets, which I respect, but this hasn't been the tradition. It has improved, but Maja likes your Elizabeth Bishop and"—he pauses and searches the ceiling again—"Castillo. Ana Castillo?"

Chaun looks impressed. "She's from Chicago."

"So," Matic says, pinching at his chin. "I am meeting an American poet and forgiving citizen. You are meeting a mountain guide." He corrects himself with a raised finger. "Former. And excuse me now for asking. Please tell me if this is a wrong question. A stereotype."

We're bracing.

"You two are what? Forty. You're young. Slovenia is not exactly known as the destination for gays. I mean, Ljubljana has a pride parade, but you could fit in maybe two buses the number of people who walk."

I jump in. "This is Chaun's idea. I wanted Florida."

"And? Why aren't you there by yourself instead of here together? You're married, not shackled."

"Because I only get a couple weeks a year. . . ."

Matic shakes his head and laughs dubiously. "Tell me, boys. I assume you live in the same house. How many hours a day do you spend together?"

"Too many," Chaun says, smiling broadly.

"Maybe seven or eight. More on the weekends. A lot more."

"And the two weeks you have a year for vacation you want to spend even *more* time together? How do you make yourself new and interesting if you always experience the same things?"

Chaun nods at the proposal but now wears a skeptical expression, giving it full exposure by raking his hair away from his face. Using a thick fry as a pointer, he softly jabs toward Matic.

"Who says new and interesting is the goal? What about comfortable?" This from the Queer Riot poet.

"Bah! Tonight, Maja and I will meet up at home and I will tell her about you two and how I was offensive and friendly. And she will tell me that I don't learn. She will tell me about Lake Bled and probably some lost tourist she gave unwanted help to and I will tell her she doesn't learn. We will have a drink and it will be a good night. If it's a very good night, well . . ." He winks. "We could not tell these stories if we are always together."

This strikes me both as a pernicious sentiment and something that makes entire sense. What if it were Chaun here alone at a trout restaurant with Matic, and I was thousands of miles away in Florida, I don't know, chatting with some similarly old dude ordering me drinks? What if we had stories to tell each other when we got back to Chicago? The waitress comes out and asks to remove the Jurassic mess of our plates, but we are still picking. Matic thanks her in English and adds something in Slovene.

"No more beer," I say.

He waves me off. "Of course not. You will be surprised." He stands and lifts his glasses to his forehead as if for the first time truly putting us in focus. "My new friends. I must be in Ljubljana tonight. It is fair to say that I have harmed and delighted you. Welcome to Slovenia!" We watch as he clomps out to his sparkling, blue-tanked motorcycle, slips on his helmet, and saddles up. Just before roaring off, he offers a two-finger so long, which we return.

Chaun and I sit looking at each other, listening to the motorcycle trail off, but not saying anything. There is nothing remarkable about the brown of Chaun's eyes, yet, his black eyebrows and lashes, the whites, all seem set perfectly as if for a masquerade ball. We have been together a long time. Not epically long, not show-up-on-the-local-news long. But still, it's longer than I ever thought possible when I was a teenager. Even in my twenties. My parents have been married nearly fifty years, and Chaun's almost as long. We are supposed to become them. Isn't that what we fought for? In weeks I'll have left my job and Chaun may be disowned. The Queer Riot poet and his stay-at-home husband.

The waitress comes out to take our plates. "Matic," she volunteers, "he comes twice, maybe three times a season. But he usually stays at his table with a book. He likes you, I guess."

I subtly elbow Chaun and check our waitress for insinuation, but she is all about clearing the table. "Have you ever met his wife?" I ask.

"Only a few times." She chuckles, hands full. "She tells *him* to order trout. But they laugh a lot and stay long. Once, two dinners."

She turns, loaded down, and as she walks away, tosses back, "He's ordered for you our potica."

Chaun shakes his head, smiling begrudgingly. "Land of poetry," he says, and then, after a pause, "You might have stuck up for me when our friend was saying that racist, homophobic horseshit."

"I'm not sure about the homophobia." Chaun is incredulous, lifting a flat palm to my face. "And besides, if I intervened I'd just be confirming his stereotype that I'm the top in our marriage."

"Weak," Chaun says. "'So much that is weak has survived and lives out its long wondrous days with only the least of annoyance.' That's Greg Kuzma."

"Now that we've established I'm weak," I say as the waitress approaches with whatever Matic ordered for us, "I hope you feel better." We are not at an impasse. By the time we get back in the car we will be talking about Matic and trout and our next destination and we will know exactly what the other one is about to say because we do everything together. And at the right moment, maybe I'll slip in that I'm taking a trip, alone, to the Florida Keys. And that I want Chaun to go somewhere fabulous so that I can hear all about it.

"This is potica. Cake. Our version." The waitress sets two large brown-and-white-swirled slices in front of us, the same stuff I thought was marble rye. Chaun asks for the check and makes a signature gesture with his right hand. "Americans always do this," the waitress says, half rolling her eyes. "Anyway, your check"—and here she mimics Chaun's gesture with a smile—"is paid."

"This has been one fucking weird day," Chaun says after the waitress walks away. "Wait till we tell Chuck and Shara."

"For sure," I say. "Exactly."

Chaun cuts into the potica with his fork and raises the piece as if to toast. "Shall we?"

"I'm full," I say, which is absolutely not true. "And *don't* tempt me. Tell me about it later?" Not eating cake might be the best part of the day, I decide. In front of us are the dozen or so rectangles of red-and-white-checkered tablecloths and, beyond that, the pine-filled pass and jagged silhouettes of gray mountains in the distance, the kind of view one wants to spend a long time describing to someone who's never been here.

NOVELLA

with pillow mint

i, kid:
intervention won

The finest work of any artist is that which saves his life.
—Rudigger Holtz, trans., *The Death of Compromise*

Onward, Christian Monkeys

Complications. That is why a middle-aged man is lying in bed being taken care of by his seventy-seven-year-old aunt while I wonder if there will be a wedding, if there will ever be a cow, if I am redeemable, and why bother? That is why, as Auntie stands over me praying for my recovery, thanking her lord for the omelet, which sits tantalizingly close on a tray across my waist, that is why I am thinking about whether or not, since we are blood relatives, whether I am doomed to inherit her bulldog jowls, whether I will keep my hair and if it will stay as naturally dark as hers. I never got to see my own parents age, though it's not hard to imagine my mother's face in Auntie's. I am thinking, too, about how there should be a law against putting bacon in front of someone right before prayer. And short of sawing my leg off above my knee, wondering how many minutes until my next painkiller. How many days or weeks until Auntie is gone, and I can have a drink even though that's what put me here in the first place?

I am not listening to her prayer. I mean, I get the gist, that He is responsible for all good things, I am dreading what will happen next, what has already established itself as a pattern. I will eat Auntie's exceptional food—I give credit where credit is due—and Auntie will roll the television in, sit next to me, and we will watch a woman with tangerine hair read from the Bible and cry into a wadded tissue.

"She has the Holy Spirit with her," Auntie says this morning. For days now we have been watching this woman sob as she wanders the gold-gilt set with its throne-like chairs. She does not look into the camera, but instead, speaks to a congregation we cannot see, she keeps letters from children tucked in the pages of her blue Bible and comes across them almost by accident. "1 Corinthians 15:44. It is sown a natural body; it is raised a spiritual body. There is the natural body, and there is a spiritual body." She turns the page. "Oh, a little note from José in Nicaragua thanking us for the medicine." But today she is not asking us for money for José, she asks for money for a new satellite. A phone number stays locked in the lower center of the screen. All the while Auntie listens and nods. She is filled with hope. I'm trying to keep my omelet down.

Auntie the devoted. Devoted to my mother. Regular Election Day volunteer. Lived with Barbara for seventeen years. Then Barbara left on mission to Africa. Auntie refused to join her. Ever since it's understood nobody must bring up Barbara. Auntie has her missions here. Aplenty.

I could distract myself with the books stacked like knee-high totems along the four walls of the room. They are a testament to a time when I used to read, actually referred to myself as a reader. But when it got to the point that I could remember starting books but none of the content, I knew I had to make a choice between alcohol and reading. My response was "Cheers!" I'd go through life, I decided, quoting from the library in my head but not add one more book to the shelf. And so I sit here quietly, giving Auntie false hope that one of her religious programs will somehow reach me.

One might have imagined I was destined for great religious things from my infancy. At our church Christmas pageant I was the swaddled Christ child in ten-year-old Bethany Crandle's (AKA Mary's) arms, the same Bethany Crandle who became my babysitter a few years later, taught me the word "twat," and split soda pop with me by cramming my glass with ice while she had hers without, always making a point to show me that she poured the glasses even. As if she imagined Mary feeding Jesus lentils from the smallest bowl filled to the brim, while she ate solemnly from the bottom of a giant pot. "I do without so that you might have enough," plump Mary would have said. Bethany was far from the mother of the savior, and as it turned out, playing baby Jesus was the peak of my religious career.

From behind, as Auntie watches television, she looks practically the same as she always has, except grayer of skin. Same complicated bun, tight braids coiled into a large mollusk attached to the back of her head. Same bovine shoulders, Olympic in breadth. And she smells like apples, as she always has. And if you want to know how sure I am of this, how precise her sweet scent, warm a few slices of Braeburn in a buttered skillet and that is Auntie. As a child in her lap, I would secretly scan her, sniffing inconspicuously to see just how the scent was possible, especially because she is famous for saying that "perfume is for prostitutes and Catholics." But nothing, not her fingertips, not her hair nor elbows, smelled any different than the whole. Apples all.

This morning, as overproduced religious music careens out of the television, Auntie and I are warmed by a white parallelogram of light from the window, and if I could sit up just a bit higher, I'd see the artichoke fields in mid-growth. Say what you will about Los Angeles, but when those fields along Wilshire Boulevard, where the Wong clan farmed artichokes for sixty years, when they were threatened by development, the city and its voters passed a bond to buy all ninety-seven acres and preserve them as an agricultural park. The "city of whores and terror" that Gavin Nabe wrote about made a stab at redemption. And so, outside my window, where my house borders Wong Family Fields, I can see, when I'm mobile and sober, rows and rows of jagged, silver-leafed, prehistoric-looking artichoke plants.

"By the way," Auntie says, turning to me. "I've taken the liberty of storing some of your products. I'll need to replace them when I go to the store."

"Products?"

"The Magic Sizing, for one. The air freshener."

"Wizard?" I ask, feeling sudden potpourri-scent withdrawals. But before Auntie answers with the litany of products she will not use, I understand what's going on, recall the near rage she flew into when I was eight and playing Merlin with her daughter, Esther. I pretended with my twig wand that I was changing her into different animals, each of which she performed eagerly, rhino, monkey, kangaroo, sea bass. And Auntie was having none of my evil presence, nothing that hinted at the supernatural, nothing that could possibly offend God or invite Satan into her home. Auntie was vigilant to say the least. She used to tell us, "Don't bother locking the doors if you're just going to let the Devil in through the window." Summer days spent at her house were scrubbed clean of *Bewitched* and *I Dream of Jeannie* reruns. Yes to Abbott and Costello in *Buck Privates*. No to *Abbott and Costello Meet the Mummy*.

And so this itself is a kind of rerun, Auntie staring at me with unblinking blue eyes waiting for a challenge while I mentally scan my cupboards, thinking of anything that might say *Works like magic*, and knowing with certainty that my Lucky Charms are packed away, but also wondering if the "miracle stain remover" will make it under the radar despite what must, in Auntie's mind, be a sacrilegious slogan.

"Okay," I say. "Get whatever you need." Who am I to argue in my hobbled condition? One knee replaced, and an ankle so thrashed I swear the doctor crossed her fingers the last time she examined me at the hospital.

Auntie nods, an irritating tincture of triumph in her smile, as if, I'm thinking, she's poised to say at any minute, "You'll thank me for this someday." But what she actually says is something far more tragic and disturbing. "And I've removed the alcohol from the house. All twenty-seven bottles. Really, Thomas, twenty-seven. I pray for you."

"If prayer actually worked, I'd be sober."

She titch-titches me and turns back toward the television. I am immediately lost in the idea of a shot of vodka, or any of the other twenty-six bottles banished to the garage—I'm *hoping* the garage. But I'm living in the land of cold turkey (but not Cold Duck) as long as Auntie is here and I'm not supposed to walk on my own. On television the tangerine-haired woman is in a pretaped segment walking through a garden. But something's off. The jungle-like trees are alive with small gray mammals. "What the hell is that?" I ask.

Auntie shoots me a disapproving look. "That," she says, "is the monkey aviary."

I don't bother to question her on the description, and besides, if it weren't for the fact there are dozens of spider monkeys leaping through the branches, it does indeed look like a large, very large, aviary, a dome of thick, green wire mesh tall enough to contain full-grown fishtail palms and an enormous barely leaved tree that looks like it's taken quite a beating.

"They broadcast a lovely service from there every Sunday," Auntie says. "It's a rescue place when people can't handle their monkeys anymore. I wrote them a check once. Very nice services."

"You realize we're talking about monkey church?" As I say this, they shoot to a clip of about twenty people inside the aviary sitting on folding chairs in front of a waterfall. A man in a suit and tie stands in front of them with a Bible, their simian friends sitting and eating chunks of fruit at the feet of the congregation. The tangerine-haired woman is doing a voice-over. "And here," she says, "is where the monkeys seem to have a sense of the presence of the Lord."

I laugh. I laugh a lot but Auntie isn't in on it. She turns to me sternly and though I know she'd never hurt me, I can't help feeling vulnerable. If she wanted, she could slam my knee, twist my ankle, and I'd be done. Instead, she does what she has always done, fixes eyes on me, blue ice cradled in wrinkles and all the more powerful for it. Her side of the family immigrated from Ireland in the mid-1800s, a tough lot then. Just as tough now.

The woman interrupts us. "Of course, monkeys can't know our Lord. I feel sorry for them." She air quotes. "'Evolution' will never make that happen. And isn't it sad that so many people are as bad off as monkeys?"

"Thomas," Auntie says, snapping, erasing my age, "your problem is you just can't find hope or joy in anything. Your mother and father, God rest their souls, are looking down from Heaven right now and shaking their heads at what you've become. What you really need in your life is Jesus."

"Or something," I toss off, stinging a bit at the mention of my parents and expecting one of Auntie's well-rehearsed and oft-imparted lectures on the Christian life.

But this time it doesn't come. Instead, she stands and takes a slow, frustrated breath.

"Yes," she says. "Or *something*. That would be a start."

With This Ring

She said no. This was a year ago. Didn't even give me the courtesy of jilting me at the altar, just set down the glass of wine she'd been nursing all evening—Gloree could drink from a thimble and never get to the bottom—looked at me sadly, and shook her head. "I can't, Thomas."

Maybe if I hadn't asked we'd still be together now. But it was three years and I was certain of the answer. So I looked at her in a way I hadn't since we first met. Suddenly she was a stranger again, a beautiful stranger who wasn't looking me directly in the eyes. And so, it was the part running scalp-white through her dark pin curl hair that stared back at me. If it were a river, it would spill out into the pale gulf of her forehead, the sea of her face that she was hiding from me.

"Why?" I asked finally, pulling back the velvet box that I still held between us, a black hole in my hand sucking all the energy in the room.

Gloree looked up clear-eyed, both of them densely green and purposeful. "Because," she began, "I can't spend my life married to a project."

And that's it. She didn't elaborate at first and I knew precisely what she meant, though I didn't see it coming. A guy doesn't propose if he isn't sure of the answer. And if Gloree thought of me as a project all that time, she didn't let on. But the truth is, I was, I am, I suppose. For a minute or two we sat quietly, one of the few times in our relationship I remember an awkward silence. Though I'm sure in some of my less sober moments she told me plenty of heartfelt things that are lost to time and her own memory. And while we sat there silently figuring out what this all meant, I wanted to ask her about those moments, what she had said that maybe now I could hear clearly. But to ask would be to admit that she was right, that I am a project, and I didn't need the repetition. What I needed was a drink, something stronger than the cabernet.

"Thomas," she said after a while, arranging the black strap of her cocktail dress, which all through dinner seemed determined to shimmy off her thin shoulder. "Thomas, this is very hard. Of course it makes sense that you asked. We're supposed to be together; I believe that. But I just never see any change in you. The drinking. You won't get rehab . . . and you never go back to your real canvases anymore, just all that awful stuff you get paid to do."

I set the ring box on the homemade coffee table, a glass top resting on four pillars of unread books, and swallowed the remainder of my wine. In that second, Gloree's face was blocked out by the round pedestal of the glass itself, a suddenly familiar eclipse.

When it was clear there were just no more words, I saw Gloree to the door where we were immediately netted by the sweet aroma of night-blooming jasmine. On any other evening it would have been romantic, but Gloree simply kissed me on the cheek without sound, a sad punctuation that I would feel for a long time. As she turned to go, I noticed how her hand was so luminous against the small black purse with its silver clasp, how her fingers were strong and bright, and still unadorned. We did not say good night. I simply closed the door and walked back to where we'd been sitting. On the coffee table surrounding our wine were the rings and crescent stains on glass that came after an early jostled pour. Our separate clusters were distinct, tight, not one of them reaching out, breaking toward those opposite. Beneath the glass, at the corners, the titles of the topmost books of each supporting column seemed random, without irony or a sign from the world that life would be okay—*Querelle*, *30 Days to a Thinner You*, *Gaudí's Barcelona*, *Swimming the Witch*. After a couple more glasses of wine, I picked up the tabletop and turned it over so I could preserve the dried rings for just a while longer. From the underside they suddenly looked like fossils on display.

Hey, Zeus Is Coming!

Only at first, it's hard to read the name in its Spanish pronunciation. Jesus. But it's not the character from the Bible. At least I don't think so, since it's unlikely that the son of God would send me a letter on blue stationary with a strawberry border. And it's even more unlikely that a letter from Christ would come to *me* of all people. *Besides*, I can't help thinking, *where would he get the stamp? Would he waste a miracle? Turn paper into postage?* I'm thinking of this name, Jesus, in the vein of Juan, or more accurately José and Jorge. Hey Zeus. But then I have to decode the brief letter, note really. And while Auntie is out of the room, presumably conspiring to further purify my home, I've remembered a little something tucked in the drawer of my nightstand. Airline vodka. Seven of them to be exact. The only reason I'll ever be glad I flew to Albuquerque. A steward's apology for dropping a bag on my head, despite his own advice to be cautious about opening the overhead compartments "as contents may have shifted during flight." I suck one of the life givers down and conceal the bottle back in the drawer with its healthy little brothers. Rejuvenation. The note says:

> Sorry for the delay. Will arrive soon. I appreciate the space. I hope everything will change. Your friend, Jesus. PS Happy to help out.

It is either a joke, for which I'd suspect my aunt or, more

likely, the result of one of my not-uncharacteristic blackouts. One of my drunken promises, which, frankly, I always keep not out of conscience, I suppose, but more of a code of honor. This poor guy probably met me at some party when I was lit on cheap vodka and told me a sob story about needing a place to crash. I can imagine myself—and when you don't have memory, imagination is the only substitute for recall—"You know, buddy," I'd say, "I gotta place you can stay there in my place."

At least, this is how I've been told it happens. This is what the woman "reminded" me of when she showed up with her parrot and all his paraphernalia. She, off to Brazil for two months, I—who knew that when drunk I could pass myself off as a great bird lover?—apparently promised to house the creature. Two months of bird talk, half of it "Hi, Mommy" and "Out!" And the feather plucking as its anxiety grew.

And then the time I received a two-hundred-dollar check in the mail with a note. *Thanks for the loan, you're a lifesaver. Added an extra twenty. The drinks are on me. God bless, Becky.* Who Becky was, I have no idea, but yes, God bless her. The twenty bucks was 1.5 Manhattans including tip. That I remember.

So here's this note from Jesus and apparently I've offered him some space. What are the possibilities? An artist? Meth-lab operator? Whatever the case, he will show up and I will invite him in because that's the way Pops showed me, though neither of us realized I was taking notes. A man who keeps his promises is in control. Which is why the holidays were the best when I was a kid, Pops tight on eggnog or hot toddies, doling out promises of trips and house projects for the coming year. In one five-year stretch Mom transformed our little stucco home based solely on Pops's soused optimism for the coming twelve months. And never once did Pops renege, not on the Grand Canyon, or the pool, not on New York or the wall-to-wall green shag carpeting in the living room. Pops always with a smile, off to work every morning in his white short-sleeved shirt and black tie, back every evening with the same smile and the familiar endearment for me. "Boy, fix your old man a drink."

Well, once, but I don't count that time. Pops was pretty tight, and watching television when an insurance commercial came on. There was a voice-over while the camera panned, a farmer standing in front of a bunch of cows, the black-and-white dairy kind, and I mentioned to Pops that I'd never actually seen a cow in person.

"You know what I'm going to do, boy?" He gestured with his drink in hand, which was his form of oath taking. "I'm going to hunt up a dairy and find you a cow."

So that was the one, the only promise he didn't keep. I didn't bother reminding him because I wasn't really sure I wanted to see a cow. I still haven't. Not in person.

So, I score Pops at 100 percent. And in that way, I am like him. I do what it takes no matter what it takes *from* me. I look again at the note from this Jesus guy, whoever he is. The handwriting is slim but readable, nothing that suggests serial killer. I have no recollection of him. None. But he clearly has a recollection of me and that's all I need to know. And in that PS he suggests I asked for something, for some kind of assistance. What, I'd like to know. For now, I guess, he holds all the cards, my business card to be precise. I would have given it to him in my stupor, on one side, my contact info printed over the oil painting likeness of a Doberman with the liberty of a few blue-and-red highlights here and there, on the other side, my name and occupation.

Dog Portraiture
By Tom Layton Wills
Immortalize Your Pet!

You've Come a Long Way, Baby

In *The Eternal Light of Yesterday*, Marquessa Croix wrote, "Great cities are like damaged children." When I first came across that line in her book I immediately thought of Los Angeles, a city nursed on pleasure but somehow never satisfied, cranky, ready for naptime but refusing to go because sleep is where we remember what really happened to us.

Sure, I thought that. But I wonder now. So much has changed for the better, as if the city was marched off to therapy or just placed on some intense medication. We've gotten out of our cars, for one thing. That, thanks to the blessing of a critical mass of lower-income voters, who out of forced habit and conscience gave us real mass transportation, three bonds in fifteen years. Now, on the most oppressively hot days, instead of exhaust, we smell eucalyptus and sage. Electric bus and rail, the latter integrated into the cityscape so well it's hard to recall when it wasn't there, not a grid dividing LA in chunks, but a suture really, healing.

And this coming from someone struck by one of our new buses. Sideswiped, actually. My fault for teetering into the street after an evening out, alcohol my double-edged sword that night, floating me into the street, yes, but also softening me up for the blow, the difference of a fist hitting a pillow or a pane of glass. Though my knee and ankle might have something to say about my positive spin.

Spin. While I convalesce this is pretty much what my mind does. Tries to get out of bed, out of the room, out of the house even though I'm bound here, Auntie the dungeon master bringing me God and peach pie, the doses torturously favoring the It.

But my mind is on this city right now because we are at a turning point. As good as things are, we are on the precipice of going back to the way things were. Some people have already forgotten the days when we had a gas station on every street corner, when the charred hills and filthy sky looked like a freshly poured black and tan. And now, the greenbelts that wind through the city to the ocean, not green like lawn green, but more of a chaparral gray-green. Restoration. Big fat swaths of natural habitat running through Hollywood, Compton, Culver City, and Sherman Oaks in the Valley. Who would have ever guessed we'd get the Valley back? Mule deer and bobcats walk along the fences of our backyards now, and if they want, they can make it all the way to the Pacific. And sure, every now and then a mountain lion snatches a pet or toddler, but I like to think of them in a cost-benefit kind of way.

Now, we have three twenty-four-hour television channels that show every bird and mammal wandering through these new spaces. True, it makes us feel like we're doing nature a favor. Every ten minutes or so the view switches to a new stretch of corridor so that in the course of about an hour and a half a viewer can visually travel from mountain to ocean. Depending on the channel, on a good day, you might see tule elk, turkey vultures hopping nervously around a small carcass, deer, and every sort of small mammal that scurries through the brush with the same randomness a water drop travels down the side of a beer glass. Though it can be mesmerizing watching these stretches of alternately static and kinetic space, I refuse to watch after sundown when the night-vision video turns every nocturnal animal into a glow-eyed vampire.

When I was a kid, nature was what Marlin Perkins showed us from his office on *Mutual of Omaha's Wild Kingdom* reruns. Nature was in Africa, I thought. Definitely not outside our house, unless you count the Mustangs, Cougars, and Colts—and possibly the Thunderbirds if you're not a purist. Horsepower.

Nature was the crappy birdhouse I built in my one year of YMCA Indian Guides. We got kicked out. It was our turn to hold a meeting. The host dad always arranged an activity, usually one that ended up excluding the sons from all the good parts. When we made the drum we couldn't go near the molten lead nor touch the hide, had to stand back from the leather-burning tool when we made belts, had to get back, get back, when they burned our Indian names into wood plaques, had to stand off while our fathers argued about the best way to make a campfire. Our dads were latent pyromaniacs.

When it came our turn to host, Pops promised me he had something good, something the kids could do. So they all came over on one of those summer nights that doesn't cool off. There was Big Bear and Little Bear, Big Cougar and Little Cougar, Big Eagle and Little Eagle, Big Hawk and Little Hawk, Big Buck and Little Buck. Pops and I were the Owls, Big and Little respectively. Yes, I too slap a hand to my forehead at the disrespect. After the adult Indian Guides got done talking about war and transistor radios, we had our prayer and then Pops took us out to his workshop, the garage really, graveyard of aborted projects, things he never actually made promises on—a half dozen unfinished model cars, Mom's disemboweled vacuum cleaner, a ceramic mermaid that Pops bought at a yard sale and that Mom insisted have at least a bikini top painted on. "Or clam shells. Something!" she'd yelled.

Pops opened the garage door, the streetlights buzzing already, sending down beams that made me think of alien abduction. I wonder what we looked like to the neighborhood, this circle of savage natives, we with our headbands accessorized with single chicken feathers, faux-leather vests fringed at the bottom for authenticity, plastic-bear-claw necklaces, and the keenest detail of all, denim bell-bottoms. All of us standing among the suburban wreckage of my father's garage, responding with silent reverence to the tribal drum we'd made at our second meeting, courtesy of Big Eagle's knowledge of smelting lead and tanning rabbit hides.

Okay, me. I'm one of those people from elementary school recognizable even after twenty years. Not as pudgy to be sure, but really it's the same floppy hair, same hazel eyes surrounded by just enough white to always make me look a little surprised, and now, a lot bloodshot. But still, somehow I come off as that roundish kid just this side of puberty. Perhaps the one difference all my fellow Littles would notice now is the glass tumbler in my hand, never empty and yet always ready for a refill.

On the night of that meeting, Pops was bright-eyed, entirely sober, though still a bit red-faced and maybe slightly out of step with his pinkish Hawaiian shirt and sharply parted hair. But through his eyes, he had planned a very special meeting and couldn't wait to get to the activity. His anticipation rose visibly with each stage of the meeting. First, we passed around the wampum bag, where most of us made our offering with a shrug and the word "chores," though we were supposed to more thoroughly account for how we'd worked for the money. Most of us, of course, got it slipped to us minutes before the meeting so as not to embarrass our fathers.

Most of us, we of the Little menagerie set, tried to get the wampum offering over with, except Little Hawk, AKA Gordon Kelm, a porky little kid with one bucktooth side by side with a smaller tooth that had never fully grown out. Little Hawk, as at every meeting, couldn't resist the opportunity to tell some stretched-out tale of how he'd come by his wampum. That night, his fifty cents given over was the result of monitoring his elderly neighbor's lawn for poo left behind by inconsiderate dog walkers. And though Gordon's stories were always a bit disturbing, mostly we hated to hear him talk because after each sentence he slurped at his front teeth to suck back the bubbly spittle that collected there. "She was very thankful," slurp. "And she promised me cookies next time," slurp. And so on, sometimes followed by a sleeve wipe when the buildup was too great for the suck back.

We pushed our way through the meeting, Pops cutting nearly everyone short, as politely as possible, clearly anxious to get to the activity. His excitement wasn't lost on anyone. Big Buck, who'd early on established his preference for procedure, kept raising one black eyebrow in irritation, a furry boomerang riding one side of what I thought had to be the world's fattest head. "Now, Big Owl," he says, finally, "I'm not sure we're giving these little braves enough time to complete their scout reports." Of course, he'd waited until Little Buck had the talking stick and was telling about how they'd cleaned wads of maggots out of their trashcans. Fortunately, his son wasn't as invested in the story as his father had hoped and the tale ended with the phrase, "It really stank."

When at last it was time for Pops to bring out our activity, I was particularly anxious to see what he'd come up with and he looked like he was about to burst, like a kid who got paid by his older brother not to snitch about his afterschool smoking. Pops raised his arms, Humpty Dumpty now in a leather vest. "Boys," he said, "the red man gave us many gifts. He joined us at the first Thanksgiving. He brought us corn and animal hides." Pops paused for effect, looking each of us in the eyes. This was before drink had reddened his nose. Here, he was bright and focused, a once-a-month Indian, Big Owl with a safe little job, a safe little wife, and a safe little mortgage. A white guy who liked to say we had distant Cherokee ancestry. Years later I paid to find out that we do not. "Now the thing is," Pops continued, "them Indians knew a man had to have more than a full belly and a warm body. They knew a man had to have something to settle the nerves too."

At this, the other Bigs began to get nervous. Big Buck secured his son by the shoulders as if bracing him for something. An evening breeze sifted into the garage, rocking the dusty fork-and-spoon mobile suspended from a rafter. The hammered-flat-cutlery-and-fishing-line creation was part of Pops's short-lived home-crafts phase. Now he had a new hobby, apparently, one he hadn't yet shared with my mother and me. As our tribe looked on, Pops rolled a squeaky, sheet-covered cart—Mom's good pink carnation pattern that we kept for company—into the center of the garage. The other kids were looking at me for a clue as to what could possibly be in store for us. That tableau is pinned to the corkboard of my mind. A bunch of white kids pretending to be Indigenous people. But not for the first time. Starting in kindergarten hadn't we all donned construction paper feather headdresses at Thanksgiving? Not one of us, though, was ever asked to cosplay an Indigenous person enslaved and forcibly converted by Junípero Serra. Surprise!

"Boys," Pops said, "the Indian was self-sustaining and we are going to learn his ways." With that, Pops flipped back the sheet, the pink wave an impressive curl silently collapsing on the garage floor.

Not a word. We were staring at a pile of dark-brown something. Burned leather? Smoked fish filet? We looked at my father who was beaming, his smile defining his cheeks, each side punctuation dense and round as a plum. "Tobacco, boys!" he said. "Nothing was more important than the old peace pipe." He'd had it sent from South Carolina, fully cured tobacco leaves there for our educational pleasure.

"My God, Big Owl," Big Hawk screeched. "You can't teach these boys to smoke tobacco." The other Big animals chimed in with a kind of confused agreement.

My father shook his head and adjusted his feather, somehow

knowing that it was leaning to the left. "Braves, this isn't about teaching our kids to smoke. *We'll* do the smoking, of course."

Maybe it was the somewhat sweet smell of the tobacco, or the way the yellowness of the garage light cast our dads into sepia moods, or maybe it was just that all our fathers smoked, but their immediate concern for our lungs was trumped by the idea of filling their own. And then again, maybe it was just my father's convincing tone. Maybe that night he could have said, "I'm going to teach you boys how to take candy from strangers," and the other fathers would have gone along with it. Pops took out a little pamphlet from his back pocket, gave us all pairs of scissors, and we were off, snipping up a storm. We weren't men yet, but certainly, at that moment, we could call ourselves Marlboro boys.

Titty Twister

One thing I've learned from alcohol is just how imprecise the world is, how much room for error. Try this experiment. Do three shots of whiskey and wait fifteen minutes. Then drive to the store. Ninety-nine out of a hundred times you'll come back with your bread and milk without incident. Maybe nine hundred and ninety-nine out of a thousand. The point is, as much as we aim ourselves toward precision, believe that we're refining society toward attainable perfection, the more we understand that our natures will always accept the necessity of unpredictability, the need for a little flexibility. This is why we aren't bisected on the vertical by elevator doors, why we attach "ish" to meeting times. This is what Carol Maxley alludes to in *Quixotic Quickness*. "Arrive," she says, "but without the stench of eagerness." We are a nation of yellow lights. If this world were not kinetic, was black and white, there would be green—go, red—stop, and no intermediary. But intuition, reality, enforces the need for the middle option.

This flexibility, I'm beginning to understand , is how Christians use forgiveness, because a religion full of grudge holders couldn't survive if all the sinners were simply cast out. And in a nifty bit of dual functionality, acts of forgiveness are like earning stripes. Which now, given Auntie's presence, seems like a terrifically liberating concept, an escape hatch, the valve on a pressure cooker, the knowledge that all cannot be lost, ever. Because existence of forgiveness implies the existence of transgression and the two are mutually dependent. Room for error.

Now, days after she has exiled my alcohol, Auntie stands at my window holding a stack of books she's been threatening to move since she arrived. She is more than a little upset, because this morning I've forced her to contemplate forgiveness. Sunlight accents her dark hair with a bright corona, and though I know how thick bodied she is, today, for some reason, the white daisies freckling her modest pink dress make her look almost vulnerable. For a long time she does not speak, but I know what she is thinking, know that she was not pleased to find the glass bones of my minibender, my little airline bottles empty and cozied up to me on the bed like kittens. A few of those and the pain medication was even too much for me, apparently.

"That boy is at it again," Auntie says, prolonging the moment. "I've met his mother. Nice woman." She is speaking about my new neighbors, a family that moved in next door two days before I got hit. Mother, a young son, and a wheelchair-bound father. The Yeung family. My house sits much higher than theirs, so I understand Auntie's view as like being a bird on an elevated branch. I'd meant to complain about the awful plywood ramp they recently installed but then, bam, a crushed knee and ankle later and I may have to ask them for some references for my own ramp.

"Is he watering?" I ask, referring to a behavior I've also noticed, especially since they haven't officially moved in yet.

"What else? That dear boy takes bucket after bucket across the road and douses those last scraggly artichokes." Wong Family Fields.

"Baptizes?" I try to sound playful but all I get are Auntie's eyes. If brimstone came in blue, that'd be her stare.

Auntie moves away from the window toward the bed, standing above me with a hands-on-hips take-no-prisoners stance. Her daisy dress suddenly takes on the aspect of hundreds of judging eyes, their yellow cores intensely still and focused on a sinner. "Thomas, I spoke to my pastor this morning about your problem. He tells me not to be an enabler. So, I love you for Jesus. . . . And you are a drunk."

I search for a response, something like the cute things I used to say to Pops and Mom when I knew I was in it deep. Things that sounded too smart for a kid like, *I'm not the manufacturer, just the distributor*, and, *I only did it so you'd be able to tell my future wife what a handful I was.* I try to reaffirm my kid look, bright precocious eyes, irresistible smile, but today, I'm coming up empty. I shift in bed and the disturbed bottles mew at my waist. "A drunk? That's a bit harsh, Auntie. Alcoholic, sure. Boozer, maybe. But: Drunk?"

At that, she thumps down the books she's holding on top of the television and humphs. "I only have a short time here. Your choices are clear. Since you won't go into a program, it's God or alcohol."

"An ultimatum?" I ask. Though what I'm really trying to do is read the titles of the books, but the dull multicolored spines are not giving up their secrets easily.

"A goal from God. Get off the drink."

"Is this from the same God who turned water into wine?"

Auntie cracks a smile and the daisies let up too. "See how clever you are when you're sober?" She walks back to the window and leans on the sill. The forgiveness part.

"I can't stay if you're going to keep up this way."

I can't drink if she's going to stay. And I need her to stay. But not drink? As in ever? Why not just crank my nipples between pinched fingers? I know better than to ask these questions out loud, so I nod quietly. Auntie, satisfied, brightens in the sunlight and gestures toward the corner where she's set up my easel draped over with sackcloth just as I'd left it in the studio. Yes, I need to take up the brush again. Bills. And under that cloth awaits a cockeyed Pekingese in watercolor. I always do the ugly breeds in watercolor to take the edge off.

"Thanks," I say, "but the light's not right in here."

Auntie opens her arms to the air as if she's about to embark on a very happy yawn. "Yes, Thomas," she says, "that's precisely what I'm talking about. You need the right light." Auntie turns to leave the room, and maybe because she hasn't been back in Los Angeles long and doesn't know a good exit line, she adds, "I called Gloree and asked her to drop by."

It has been months since we've spoken and I'm more than a little startled that Auntie has Gloree's number. "What did she say?"

Auntie continues down the hall. "I left a message," she says.

So what if Gloree calls? What if she doesn't? And suddenly I'm thinking about our final night and the coffee table, afraid that Auntie has flipped over the glass and wiped away the rings left behind by our wineglasses. It's strange the things a person won't give up for someone else, and then the things we desperately cling to when the relationship is over. One is selfishness and the other desperation and right now I feel like a big lump of both.

It's Impolite to Pointillism

I have been good for a few days, though that might be simply because I've run out of surprise alcohol. There is one other surprise, however, a note in the mail today from Jesus that reads *On my way.* I wish it was a note from Gloree, but nothing from her yet, and I know the phone is working because I've picked it up a half dozen times to check for a dial tone, that and Mrs. Goins called to ask about how I was getting along, and as a poorly acted afterthought inquired about whether I was finishing the painting of "her Precious" anytime soon.

This is my first day out of bed, well, sort of. The physical therapist and Auntie brutalized me enough this morning so that with my walker, I can more or less stand from the bed and slump into the wheelchair. And it's a good day to take on this little trick because I'm given a reason to ignore that awful Pekingese, which even in watercolor is definitely monster-like. Two houses down, the family with the irrigating boy is officially moving into the Miller home, which is a beautiful little Victorian, blue and loopy in all the right places. How many years before I call it the Yeung home?

I know I should paint but I'd rather be distracted by the new family moving in. Chinese American, I'm sure. A man in a wheelchair, older than the woman pushing him up a makeshift ramp, and that plump little watering kid with a shag of black hair. At the sight of him I'm reminded of being slightly less fond of children than the dogs I paint. This kid seems distracted and quiet, seems less focused on the new place and more on the artichoke fields, row after row of foot-tall, jagged silver leaves shivering in occasional gusts of wind. He crosses the road and jumps a narrow culvert to the fence line across from a bleak-looking little patch of plants at the end of three or four rows. They are smaller than the rest and, from what I can tell, on their last legs.

The kid stands in front of the field for a while, his arms crossed over a belly straining against a too-small red shirt. Several times he looks back at the moving van and then again at the field as if he's formulating a plan. Finally, he walks back, dutifully looking both ways before he crosses the road and making straight for the truck. The movers are bulky and unshaven and don't pay attention to him as he stands near the truck ramp trying to get their attention. He's frustrated, I can tell, though it's possible that's my own thing since I can't hear them and don't know him. But I know when I was a kid and a bit dumpy looking myself, I may as well have been invisible. I'm frustrated for him as he scratches his bulky hair that lifts like a half-opened umbrella with each zephyr. And suddenly I realize he's not trying to get their attention; he's waiting them out.

Then, looking instantly inspired, he runs into the house and returns with an open orange snack-size bag of chips, each chip eaten gingerly and savored. Even from this distance I see that the tips of his fingers are turning the same bright color of the bag.

Finally, when the movers are both in the house the kid disappears into the truck and struggles down the ramp with two coils of garden hose looped over each shoulder. All that anticipation for garden equipment. Not a bike or soccer ball? The kid tosses down the hoses near the blockade of pomegranate and juniper on one side of the house. On hands and knees, he connects them and takes one end of the hose into the shrubbery. Backing out he drags the hose, water running full blast, across the road as far as he can where he finger pressures the stream in order to water the patch of distressed artichokes. It's a really nice thing to watch, this kid's first act in his new home is a form of rescue.

When he is done watering, the kid returns to the house where he shuts off the water and methodically retrieves the hose, looping it in perfect circles like a shiny green snake resting at his feet. There is something inspiring about watching his impulse toward productivity and it makes me think that maybe I can pick up the brush again and, at the very least, finish God-awful Precious. I'm full of a kind of energy that for a moment makes me forget my hobbled condition, but even when that comes back to me, I'm excited. I watch the kid pull up the last of the hose. His back to me, he suddenly straightens quickly, as if he's been tapped on the shoulder. In an instant he turns and looks directly toward my window, making me roll back in my wheelchair just enough to feel out of sight. The screen now pimples the scene into a kind of Seurat painting. The boy squints, faces my window, then flips me off, a very orange fingertip punctuating the gesture.

Jesus Needed a Pharmacist

I feel like a wet dishrag that Auntie is wringing out with her hands, twisting and twisting toward dehydration. I need a drink. It's been just over a week since I got hold of the airline bottles. I need a drink, but then again, the house has never been cleaner, smelling more and more like sweet lemon. The physical therapist and Auntie walk behind me as I thunk and slide and grit my teeth against the pain. The wood floors are immaculate right up to the walls, and Auntie has scrubbed the molding around the doors where the shadows of years of handprints once clung. I pay attention to these things because I'm trying not to think about what's going on below, though that comes with its own problems since I really am a baby taking his first steps again.

"Lift a little higher," the therapist says in her efficient, yet cheery, East Indian voice.

Auntie chimes in, sounding stoically Midwestern even though she moved here long ago. "Yes, Thomas. You're dragging a bit." She seems to strain either from supporting me or from the fear of failing to.

"You don't have to do this, you know," I tell her.

"It's been a long time since I've felt needed, Thomas," she says. "And lift your feet."

If pain were voltage, I'd know what it feels like to be sitting in the electric chair. I pause and stand as upright as I can, though even that act comes with its own brand of excruciation. "Ladies," I say, "it will be some time before I try out for the chorus line." We are standing in front of the decorative mirror in the hallway, which, holding my image, is anything but decorative. Even I recognize how pathetic I am, or at least look. Hair sticking out in all directions, wrinkled blue pajamas, and a flannel robe that hangs off one shoulder like it's dreaming of escape to another, better body.

"You can have your medication in the living room, Thomas," Auntie says in a tone sounding like she is offering milk and cookies to a child. Which, actually, she is. The prospect does indeed help me lift more and drag less, the therapist's hand on my back the entire way. Doing physical therapy as a means to get stronger isn't incentive enough to just get better, but doing it to get to the pain pills is. And true to her word, once I get to the recliner Auntie brings me my bottles. I read the side of one of them out loud optimistically. "Use of alcohol while taking this drug increases its effects."

Auntie eyes me and crosses her arms. "That's a warning, Thomas, not a recommendation."

"I don't think you have any idea what this feels like."

The therapist is listening and filling out a form, her black hair so styled and sharp it looks like it could buckle under her chin. "Sometimes pain can be a good thing, Mr. Wills," she says. I'm irritated by the convincing power of her accent. "You'll be able to gauge your progress by how the intensity diminishes over time. It's a good barometer of your healing."

"Well, great," I tell her, "let's just cut out all the medication so I can truly appreciate every last bit of my recovery."

"Thomas. I suppose I should remind you that Jesus was beaten and nailed to the cross and he didn't complain one bit."

"I'm flattered by the comparison," I say, saluting Auntie with a glass of water and the pills I was about to down. "And he may be here soon. Let's ask him."

She lifts an eyebrow, not understanding, but we know each other well enough to leave it at that. And later I'll find it funny to think that we were having an argument about how high I should be allowed to get. The point is moot anyway, as every place where a bottle of alcohol once stood is empty. She really had cleaned me out. The poor little things, huddled somewhere out in the garage like a band of penguins clustered against a prolonged chill in darkest winter. And I think to myself, *The real purpose of getting stronger is to rescue them*. I'll know I am recovered when I can make it down the steps and back up with at least one bottle in my hand.

When Pops came down with gout in his heel and could, would, hardly walk, he had Mom and me waiting on him hand and foot, so to speak. Not that we weren't sympathetic, but she was suspicious. So, when I was at school she told Pops she was going grocery shopping. And she quietly placed a bottle of bourbon where she was sure Pops would eventually see it. Of course, when she got home, Pops was happily toasted in his lounge chair, the bottle buddied up next to him on the end table. "See, James dear," she said, "you're not a kite snagged in a tree after all."

Lost in my fantasy heroism and perhaps feeling the bump of the medication, before I know it, the therapist says goodbye at the door.

What a job, cheeriness required even when dealing with a wreck like me. As she opens the door, sunlight rushes in like a rescuer breaking through, my eyes wincing at the brightness. And then something else as the therapist says excuse me and passes a figure in the doorway.

"Gloree," Auntie says. "You're here!"

I've Been Served

I'd known Gloree since she was ten. Back then she was the kind of girl whose mom wouldn't let her go out of the house without the right play pants with the right shoes. Back then she was Benita. Ben for short. They called her a tomboy. I can't remember a day in our younger years when she didn't arrive at school like she'd just stepped out of church. Sometimes she'd ask me to try out "girlier" names for her—Sarah, Ellen, Gloria, Theresa . . . anything but Ben. And sometimes I wonder if I fell in love with her because of one simple event when we were young. People ask, the few who know, Auntie not being one of them, and I tell them, if Gloree were still Ben, yes, I think I could love her the same, though I never got the chance since Ben's family moved just a few weeks after she rescued me. Benita, Ben, Sarah, Ellen, Gloria, Theresa, Gloree. Love the person. Ditch the hangups.

To say I was a geek in elementary school would be an understatement. Pops and Mom didn't do much to discourage it. I did all the normal boy stuff like baseball and soccer, skateboards, and books about UFOs and Bigfoot. But I also had a fascination with this fuzzy-headed man on television who taught oil painting. Mostly trees. Lots of trees and hills. Within months of watching that first show I had my own easel and paints, which wasn't so bad when I set up in front of the navel orange tree in our backyard. I had an entire grove of gloppy canvases—*Oranges at Noon*, *Oranges at Twilight*, *Oranges at Daybreak*. I was channeling Van Gogh, I think, only it was a weak signal. For some reason I got it into my head that it would be a good idea to take my supplies to school.

Unfortunately, my teacher, Mrs. Ferguson, didn't have a lame meter and she was quite excited that I wanted to use recess to paint the playground. "That's just lovely, Thomas," she said. "The other children will be so inspired." They were. Inspired to "accidentally" hit me with balls and toss bits of gravel onto the canvas. If Ben hadn't intervened I would have probably crumbled.

I was so optimistic when I first set up. Not an orange tree in sight. But there were the interesting lines the man on television had talked about and I saw right away that the swing sets and monkey bars were going to force me to use perspective like I'd never tried. I was proud of myself for seeing right away that the blacktop wasn't actually black, how the farthest reaches of the school property wavered at ground level with heat refractions. And there was the way light hit the interstices of the jungle gym, defined its three-dimensionality. But while all that was going on in my head, something quite different was happening around me. With my smudgy palette and blue smock dabbed all over the front with shades of green and orange paint, I was suddenly a lamb separated from the flock.

Gordon Mactow wandered by for the umpteenth time. "What's that supposed to be, Picasso?" He said this with the same little sneer that would get him killed in a bar fight twenty years later. Gordon was the kind of kid who got a new pair of sneakers every month. He had glistening blond hair that looked like his parents spent too much on shampoo. And of course, girls loved him.

I'd only been painting for about fifteen minutes but even then I worked fast, and maybe even faster as I felt things closing in around me. Gordon's taunting worked on me. My knees were weak and the canvas started to get blurry through no fault of the paint. But I ignored Gordon and kept going, though my strokes at that point were worthless and I'd given up on even trying to pluck out the grit and gravel.

It was hard for me to process that barrage. I was never really a popular kid in the classroom—except with teachers—nor on the playground, but bringing my paints to school didn't seem like such a big deal. With all the crazy projects Pops had taken on over the years he'd never gotten truly criticized for it. In front of me, though I tried not to show it, I saw Gordon and his buddies cooking up something. Suddenly they were playing foursquare, something they probably hadn't done since second grade. I looked around for the playground monitor, Mrs. Speck, who, as usual, was keeping track of the kids on the swings with her back to the majority of us. The foursquare game was getting rougher and I knew what was coming my way. But something kept me anchored where I was, as if I deserved all the harassment. Out of the corner of my eye I saw a large red ball headed right for me and the easel. But it never arrived. An even taller form intervened, Ben, who snatched the ball midair and threw it back so hard Gordon Mactow was on his ass. Ben stood with her arms at her thin waist in a challenge no one was willing to take her up on. It wasn't an imposing body, but her attitude was. Years later, after we rediscovered each other, when she was angry with me, Gloree would use this same pose that she had once used as my protector.

Gloree's presence in my living room is a surprise. "I have to be honest, Tommy," she says, "you look just awful." We're sitting, waiting for Auntie to bring us tea. I would have preferred coffee with a little rum and Kahlúa in it, or better, rum and Kahlúa with a little coffee. Because I know Gloree is right, I do look awful. Though I'm not bothered by that reality as much as the idea that she is thinking I've gone to hell because she broke up with me. If I hadn't made the descent before we first reconnected after a couple of decades, I'm clearly and certainly well on my way now.

For her part she doesn't look like she's lost even the slightest bit of sleep over our breakup. In her close-fitting white top and crisply pleated tangerine skirt she is the same immaculate person I've known all these years, though she calls everything she wears a costume. Some days it's work boots, a baseball cap, and dungarees. Still, always immaculate. Perhaps the only difference is what she thinks of me. While I tell her about the bus and the curb and Auntie's regime, Gloree nods slowly and narrows the space between her eyebrows as if she's listening to the most tragic story ever. I don't like this feeling, that she sees me as some sort of hopeless figure, Richard III driven to destruction by his hump.

"I knew it had gotten bad, Tommy, but really," she says as I arrive at the part where I woke up in the hospital.

"It's not so terrible," I say bravely. "I get my daily dose of Jesus from Auntie, some awfully good food, and a lot of time to think about us."

Gloree sits up straight. "Oh," she says, but it comes out more like an exhale than a word. She is clearly surprised.

I ball my hands and push myself up into the most erect position I can muster. It's never occurred to me before that sitting can be so difficult or gravity so cruel in the way it works on me both horizontally and vertically, eventually making me sag in my seat like a bored child in a church pew. "I'm not so crazy about the sermons, but it's working out okay. Auntie's got me on the wagon, so I've been pretty clearheaded. I really made some big mistakes with you and me." Even as I say this I know it's the wrong path for me to go down, not because I haven't thought about Gloree, I have, but I'm saying what I think she wants to hear. At this point the only real mistake I can honestly cop to is that I proposed without realizing that she was having doubts about us. If she had been throwing off signs, I was numb to them, literally I suppose.

"Tommy," Gloree says cautiously, "I just came to check on you, that's all. And I brought you some art supplies, in case. They're in the car. Have you painted lately?" I begin to answer but she interrupts. "Besides dogs, I mean."

"I haven't even worked on those," I tell her. She looks at her hands and picks at a cuticle, though I can't imagine what she could have been looking for: Each finger is tipped by a perfectly shaped mother-of-pearl crescent. "But maybe you could get me back into the swing of things. Make an artist of me again."

"Oh." She is done with her hands and shaking her head no. "I told you I couldn't take you on as a project and I meant it."

It's my turn to oh, only mine comes out as something like a lead ingot. "I wasn't saying we should get back together." But that's what I'm thinking, for sure. Seeing her again, knowing that she cared enough to check on me sparks all the old feelings. But I'm sure that's the problem. Seeing me sparks all the old feelings in her too, and apparently that isn't a good thing.

Auntie arrives with our tea. She's using a lime-green ceramic service that isn't anything I remember owning. "Where did you get that?" I ask as she sets the tea in front of us.

Gloree sighs. "My mother gave it to you for your birthday."

Matching Gloree's disappointment, Auntie plops onto the couch next to her and smooths out her long skirt on her lap as if she's about to have a business meeting. Both of these women have put up with a lot from me. At the very least I've helped them perfect their wit's-end looks. Auntie holds her head slightly tilted, eyes looking down her nose; Gloree searches the ceiling as if for crib notes on how to handle me this time.

"Come on, guys," I say. "I remember now. It's just that I haven't used them." I did indeed remember the birthday party, but by the time it came to gifts I was lost to the gin fizzes her father kept putting in my hands. At first it seemed like a good-natured dare on his part to have me drink something with raw egg, but when he offered me the fifth or sixth and I said sure, he turned to Gloree and said, "I thought so," as if each drink was one step closer to a realized prediction.

"Wonderful, Thomas," Auntie says. "A recovered memory. One down and how many to go?"

"Speaking of memories and Mother," Gloree interrupts, "I was visiting last week, and she'd taken a bunch of things out of the attic. She found your painting, Tommy, the one you did of the playground."

"Wow," I say, turning to Auntie, trying to muster some lightness. "It was art that brought us together . . . when we were ten."

"Thomas painted me some lovely pictures when he was young," Auntie says, tugging at the bottom of her blouse to correct some imagined rumple.

"And today I'm very well exhibited in attics throughout the state."

"As a matter of fact," Auntie says, "the one you did of the poppies in Griffith Park is still in the dining room."

I had a fairly long California-poppy period. They were kind of hard to resist, wide delicate petals of a silken orange rising out of dusty green lace. And when they go to seed a pod elongates from the stem, a fertile spear that browns and crisps and splits, spilling tiny black balls to the ground. I'd captured all these stages in my paintings. But the one that Auntie was talking about I finished when I was eighteen on the morning of my parents' funeral. I holed myself up in the studio Pops built for me in the backyard and sat in front of the canvas, a bluish early light washing over me. The painting had been in limbo for a couple of weeks. There was no emotion in it, just a sterile clump of poppies foregrounded over smoky foothills. But something about my parents' accident sent me out to the studio with an answer. I added one more flower, one I imagined was the first to bloom and had already lost one of its petals. Life is not static, I was learning.

A few weeks later when Auntie was helping me make decisions about the house, I gave her the painting and she began to cry. She understood.

Gloree, Auntie, and I drink our tea, well, Gloree and I, Auntie sips. I'm sure it isn't lost on either of them that I now smell of Darjeeling rather than whiskey exhale.

Gloree stands and looks around the room. "Well," she says, "I guess I should get going. But Tommy, I need a favor."

"Anything," I say.

"I have a client who loves everything I've done with her living room except the art over the fireplace. I've driven her to three galleries and she doesn't take to anything I suggest." Gloree digs into her purse and pulls out four photographs of the living room. It definitely has her signature on it, contemporary, but livable. Clean lines, not too much white, definitely no oak, but some dark-wood accents, a space where you could set your drink down, not worry about a coaster, and still feel like you're surrounded by class.

"That's going to be a big painting," I say, looking at the broad space above an extra-wide fireplace.

"We've decided to commission someone. She's got some ideas about what she wants."

"Sure," I say. "I can recommend a couple people."

"I already recommended someone," Gloree says, sitting back down and staring at me intensely. Auntie quietly nurses her tea, but I have a feeling she's in on it.

"Me?" I say. "I haven't done anything real in quite a while, Gloree. You know that. I'm not an artist anymore." As I say this, the bookshelf directly across the room faces me like rows of stacked, multicolored grins, as if to say, "You're not a lot of things anymore."

Gloree leans in and places her hand on my arm, which makes me feel kind of sad, sensing the charge of her touch and knowing she doesn't share the feeling with me. "Tommy, it's a lot of money and I wouldn't ask if I didn't think you were the right person. I need you."

I look at Auntie, who seems to be praying over her tea. Gloree's eyes are strong on me, seriously plaintive. If they'd arranged a pity job, I can't see it in her expression. "A poodle," I say, holding up the fireplace photo. "I see a very large, purple poodle with a green rose in its mouth."

"You read my mind." Gloree laughs. "So you'll do it?"

"I'll talk to your client and see what's what," I tell her, though I plan to be entirely unconvincing as an option.

Gloree sits back, clearly relieved. She *does* want me to do this job for real. "But Tommy," she says, "you can't screw this up. Remember it's *my* reputation as much as yours. On time and no drinking."

I try to look offended, but I know if I was in her shoes, knowing me as well as she does, I'd say the same thing. "Don't worry," I say, "with Auntie around, the strongest thing I'll have is that grape juice she gets as Communion once a month."

Auntie winks. "Yes, and he'll be lucky to get that." She wears an expression of calmness and confidence I haven't seen in a long time.

After we settle the logistics and Gloree comes back from the car with the art supplies she got me—complete with two canvases that are coincidentally the size I'd need for the commission—our little reunion is over. Gloree thanks me again and I watch Auntie see her out the door. I sit alone listening to their voices trail off as they walk away from the house. The living room is as quiet and empty as I've ever known it. I look at the blank canvases. They too seem impossibly empty. What have I done? There is no way I am going to let Gloree's client hire me, because, the truth is, at this point, all I have in me is that purple poodle and even that is a bad joke.

Jesus on Line Two

First things first, I think. I have Auntie set up my easel near the window of the bedroom and we rig up the pillows in the wheelchair so I can sit a little higher. Then we have to gently roll my extended leg beneath the easel without knocking into its back leg. It isn't the most comfortable position to paint from, especially sober, and the lowered angle of my leg makes my ankle throb, but I need to get back in the saddle for Gloree.

Back in the saddle means Auntie sitting that damn Pekingese, Precious, in front of me so I can get it out of the way. There isn't much left to do.

"You all set?" Auntie asks. She's wearing one of her church dresses and a little blue hat covered in an even lighter blue netting. This means she is going out for a couple of hours. Earlier this morning the television service we watched featured a very large guest preacher from Georgia who couldn't have buttoned his suit jacket with a bungee cord. He talked about the "different houses of the Lord" and how beautiful his church was because his congregation didn't just come to church on Sundays, but volunteered to do its upkeep during the week. I counted. Auntie offered up seventeen amens, which I knew meant she was being inspired to do something.

"All set," I say, though what I want to say is "Please don't leave. I'll watch church TV all day with you, but don't make me sit here and paint Precious."

She's arming me with snacks, juice, and a phone on top of my roll-around art cabinet, but Auntie seems to have no qualms about leaving me alone. "Oh, Thomas," she sighs, smoothing down my uncombed hair.

"Oh what?"

She pauses and looks at me sweetly, smelling of apples and kindness. "This thing Gloree wants you to do is a doorway. You're going to get better. I can feel it." With that, she is off to clean pews for the main man in her life. Though I don't know why she got dressed up to do it. But I just keep my mouth shut because she's full of hope that I can't live up to. Plus, when Gloree's client calls I will not be the man for the job. I'll make sure of it. I can't have her career resting on my shoulders or in my sloshy brain.

When Auntie leaves, I find myself staring a bug-eyed dog right in its two-dimensional watercolor face. I sit for ten minutes studying the painting, refreshing my memory as to what I was going for a few months ago. Then I look at my bed, which really needs making, all the books I should read, and my nightstand cluttered with pill bottles and tissues, a water glass. I am experiencing the first rule of producing art. The minute you sit down to do it, everything else seems much more important. I can practically hear the laundry calling to me from the hamper. And under different circumstances I might have spent the day puttering around the house (and drinking) instead of painting, but with my legs, I am a prisoner to this one activity.

Fantasizing about housework morphs into looking for gray hairs on my forearms, which is fortunate, because it makes me think about

Hank Grahm, an old man I met in my teens. Hank was a miniaturist, and when I was introduced to him, he was painting the Ten Commandments on two lima beans. Exquisite lettering on a field of green, perhaps not the same as Moses's tablets, but if he'd had the commandments in that shrunken state maybe we would have been forced to pay closer attention to them. On the day I met Hank he was working on "Thou shalt not covet thy neighbor's wife." I was less impressed with this imperative than with the fact that Hank's brushes were hairs he plucked from his arms. And this thought leads me back to my own brushes and the painting in front of me, which I decide isn't so bad.

I'd softened all Precious's worst bat-faced qualities and lightened her black muzzle a bit. But still, she doesn't have that sparkle that I know the owner sees in her. A pair of angel's wings would have worked, I suppose. With no ideas I pick up a brush, and then the phone rings, thankfully. It's Auntie, asking if I remember the name of the preacher on the television this morning. "Pastor wants to send away for a transcript of his sermon," she says, excited. I imagine her telling the story of how the preacher's congregation did all the work for the church and how her own pastor's eyes must have widened when she got to the part where the preacher, in his genteel Southern accent, talked about how sometimes the "sweet ladies" have even helped his wife give their house the once-over.

Auntie and I bat last names around a few times, Thoms, Toombs, Tims, but before we land on anything, another call beeps in on my line. "Hey, brother," the voice says, "it's Jesus." And when he speaks his name it isn't with the Spanish pronunciation. Not Hey Zeus. Geezus. Finally I'll find out what I promised this guy. I ask him to wait a second and click back over to Auntie. I can't resist. "Got to go," I tell her. "Jesus is calling."

When I come back on the line with my mystery guest, he is humming something I've never heard, his own on-hold music I suppose, kind of Gregorian without the full-on chant. "Got your note," I tell him.

"Well, brother, I'll tell you. I got to thinking I better call before I arrived to make sure the offer was still open."

"Sure, sure," I tell him, still wondering what offer it was I made. I break half a tablet of painkiller and pop it in just to give me a little bump for the painting I am about to take on.

"You never know. Sometimes people invite me into their homes and then they back out when I actually take them up on it."

I note that, apparently, he has a track record for staying with people, and wonder if maybe I just ran into some sort of contemporary hobo. And if that is true, it says a lot about the kind of parties I attend. He tells me there are a few things he needs to check on before he arrives. Outside in the artichoke fields two people in cowboy hats walk slowly between the sunny rows, stopping to bend and inspect the occasional plant. "The only thing I don't recall," I say, "is what it is you plan to do while you're here."

"I've always got people to see. And then, of course, I promised to give you a hand."

I look for cover. "Oh that, well, as it turns out, things are kind of on hold. I've had a little accident. Messed up my legs."

"Listen, brother. If you want to back out, it's cool with me. A lot of people do."

Even though I recognize that is my chance to blow him off, I still have Pops in the back of my mind. He would never have reneged on a promise. So I tell Jesus I am looking forward to having him, but that Auntie is staying with me, so the couch is all I have to offer. I think, too, I am in the mood to be distracted from painting, so an extra person in the house, a little more turmoil, will certainly do the trick. But it is more than that. The other half of my painkiller lies on the art cabinet with the little snackies left by Auntie, so I think, *What the hell.*

The longer I talk to Jesus the more I find there is something inviting and calming about him. His voice is whispery or raspy, like he'd been singing acid rock late into the night and his vocal cords haven't recovered. I find myself leaning forward as if he is sitting next to me and I am trying to get closer to the sound. After a few minutes he has me talking about Gloree and, yeah, maybe about my drinking too much. "I hear you, brother," he keeps saying. Only it isn't tossed off. It feels like he does hear every word I tell him, and I know why, even in whatever stupor I'd been in, why I trusted him the first time we met.

"It's all set, brother," he says, when my litany has dwindled down to the very moment between us and the Pekingese looming in front of me. "I'll see what I can do when I get there."

I still don't know what he plans to do, but I am certainly curious to find out. Somehow comforted when we get off the phone, I have an idea about Precious. She isn't luminous the way her owner sees her, not in this version, but the extra pill and talk with Jesus loosens me up a bit and it occurs to me that I can just apply some razor-thin clear-acrylic lines over the watercolor, and I'll have it.

Inside the art cabinet Auntie rolled in for me are all the supplies I've used to paint a couple of kennels' worth of dogs. Those, and as I reach around blindly in the back of the top shelf, a half-full, very large bottle of bourbon turned on its side, which feels surprisingly substantial and cool as I pluck it out by its neck. The pleasure and guilt of it feel like being a hunter carrying home someone else's shot-down goose. It's shocking Auntie didn't sniff out this bottle, and pretty rare that I forget about where I've stashed alcohol, but I had reason to blank on this one. The top half of it got me through the final hours of the Dinzer pit bull fiasco. He accused the portrait of his dead dog of being too literal. "Get some fierceness in him, some spontaneity, goddamn it," he yelled. A night of fang extension, cartoon swoosh lines, and a half dozen glasses later I called him back. "Your fucking dog never looked meaner."

So here I am ready to get to work on the Pekingese at last and up jumps the Devil. My hands have always been a divining rod when it comes to alcohol, so it isn't all that surprising to me that I've ended up with the happy coincidence of an empty house and open bottle.

Handsome. People don't think about how handsome dark alcohol is. I think about Auntie and my no-drinking promise to Gloree. Of course, I haven't started on her client's painting yet, haven't even talked to her, so I tell myself the meter isn't running on that promise yet. Plus, really, what can one shot hurt?

The Hair of the Dog That Painted You

Mom liked to say she was pretty good about keeping Pops on a leash when it came to his drinking, though that leash was long enough to circle the world a few times. "Oh, well," she'd casually start when someone dared to bring up the subject, "as long as he doesn't drive, there's no harm. And let's face it, we all have our vices." I heard her toss off this same line a dozen or so times when I was a kid. At each instance she stood up and offered the person something or asked them a question that seemed to me like a silent shot across the bow, though I never saw it register on anyone's face. "More coffee?" "Cigarette?" "Got any gossip?"

The only time she didn't get away with it was when she and Auntie were picking avocados from our backyard to sell at her church's annual farmers' market. Though I wasn't a fan, the fruit from that big old tree was always a hit. It was kind of a wonder in the neighborhood because when the developers built that swath of homes our avocado was the only tree that didn't get leveled in the process. As Auntie and Mom picked and talked, I was in my studio, which Pops built close to the tree but just outside the reach of its shadows. I was working on a portrait of Mom and Pops for their anniversary, which was a few months away. It was mostly complete, but at the last minute I'd decided to update their clothes a little bit since I was working from a photograph five years old. Ties had gotten wider, for one thing, and Mom wasn't wearing those beady outfits anymore. I don't know why it didn't occur to me before, but there I was, dressing my parents to look a little more up-to-date while outside Auntie decided to dress Pops down to Mom.

"Hunhun," which was what she'd called Mom since they were girls, "is James drinking a bit more than he used to?"

"About the same," Mom answered. I heard a plop to the ground, which meant one of the avocados had missed the bag at the end of her picker pole. "You know how he is. There are times when he might go for a stretch full throttle. But it averages out."

I had stopped painting and it was clear to me they weren't aware I was in the studio or Mom would've clammed up for sure. Auntie was persistent, and from the sound of it, I knew that she had stopped picking avocados. "Something's different this time, though," she said. "This morning he was fixing a bloody mary while Thomas was eating breakfast."

Mom had a shrug in her voice. "Well sure, Annie, I'd prefer it wasn't an all-day thing, but he's just going through some tough times at work right now."

"No, Hunhun. This is very different. He sat down in front of that glass and never took his eyes off it, never once acknowledged Thomas."

Mom didn't respond immediately, and I thought about Auntie's little scenario. It had happened just as she said but I never registered the moment until she mentioned it. The truth was, and maybe Mom was being intentionally blind, there were a lot of those kinds of mornings over the previous year. Pops was in deeper than he'd ever been and it happened so gradually I don't think Mom and I appreciated the change. Before, no matter how much Pops tied it on the night before, he managed to at least manufacture some interest in us before he was off to work. But I guess even Mom had trained herself out of that expectation because there were a lot of mornings where she wasn't even getting up to see us off.

That morning, Pops had his shirt and tie on, and he was just as groomed as ever, thinning hair flattened over his scalp, a hint of mouthwash wafting about before he took his first swallow from the bloody mary. But even if I'd said hello, I'm not sure he would've heard me. The day was already heaped on his shoulders and as Mom and Auntie talked it occurred to me that I'd almost forgotten how to speak to my own father.

"All I'm saying," Auntie continued, "is that maybe this time you need to speak to him."

"So what's the news with Barbara," Mom asked, in the recognizable clip that meant she was done talking.

"Independent as always. Barbara is independent." *Great loves aren't necessarily requited*, I remember thinking, though maybe not quite in those terms.

I'm not sure why, but as I sat listening to Auntie urge Mom to talk to Pops about his drinking, I was rooting for Mom to say no. I wanted her to say that he'd snap out of it on his own, that he'd soon come up with one of his big, improbable ideas that would make us all laugh. And the more we laughed the more determined he'd be to see it through until we ended up with something like the windmill butter churn he built. But Mom didn't say any of that. Instead, she was crying, and if I could have seen her and Auntie, I know they were holding each other.

"You know, Hunhun," Auntie said, taking a risk, "the problem itself doesn't start when you talk to him. It's already there or we wouldn't be discussing it now."

I looked at my painting of Mom and Pops and at the photograph I'd used as a model, in which he stood a head taller than her and she leaned in just slightly, her hand resting on the breast pocket of his green jacket. Pops was smiling, but he looked a bit pink and tired, like they'd posed for that picture at the end of a very long day. Mom, honestly, with her soft smile, looked oblivious. In my painting, besides their clothes, I'd freshened Pops up a bit, taken some of the burden out of his expression. The photographer had made Mom's face just slightly gauzy, not enough to set her in a different world than Pops but just out of focus enough to give her a dewy quality. So I sharpened that up too. I was looking at two versions of my parents, both of them altered, neither quite right, and I was coming to understand that the third version, the real one, wasn't at all the parents I was willing to paint.

i, kid: intervention too

The Knick of Late

It is late afternoon when I wake up, or stir to be more precise. My eyes focus first on my little paint table and the empty bottle of bourbon. And though I don't have any clear recollection of it, the painting of Precious the Pekingese is complete. The translucent streaks I planned, and apparently executed, are exactly what it needed, and I smile, proud that I've pulled it off even though I went under. The pain medication and bourbon put the whammy on me, and I still came out alright.

I don't revel long, though, because I am suddenly aware of the rest of the house. Silence. It occurs to me that if Auntie catches me like this I'll be in for it and I am relieved to know she hasn't gotten home yet. I tuck the empty bottle back inside the cabinet and as I close its door I immediately hear footsteps coming from the kitchen. Auntie. And unless she's left me alone thinking I was painting, I am in huge trouble. The door is shut, so there's a chance I'll get away with it. With the most plausible smile I can muster, I look up at the spot where I expect to see her face when she walks in, perhaps catch her off guard with brightness. I pat down my hair and wet a finger in my mouth to clear the sleep out of my eyes. Even if she has seen me, I think, maybe she'll let me off with a light sentence if I can show her it isn't a big deal.

The door opens but there is no face up high to meet my smile, though a foot and a half down there is. Standing in my doorway with his mussy black hair is the plump kid who flipped me off. He stands with his hand on the knob staring at me with a kind of incredulous pinch in his expression, as if I am an unconvincing wax figure. Both of us wait for the other to say something. I shrug my shoulders as if to ask him for an explanation and he shrugs back, the bottom of his T-shirt rising just enough to reveal the overhang of his belly.

"You're just as creepy up close," the kid says.

"And you're just as obnoxious." Another standoff of silence until I give in. "So, kid," I ask, "what are you doing here?"

He steps into the room but not within reach, and that feels purposeful. It isn't a gesture of fear, but more like control. The kid has assessed. I am largely immobile. He knows I can bend my elbow with a glass in my hand, but nothing is bending below the waist. He can stand right where he is and be in charge. I can't grab him by the scruff of the neck and toss him out, a fact that is painfully obvious. "That old lady slipped me some cash to sit here until you woke up. My mom said it's okay as long as I have my phone."

Auntie. She'd found me, bottle and all. I am in for it.

"So I guess I can go now. Right?"

"Wait," I say. "When did she say she'd be back?"

The kid closes his pudgy arms across his chest. "She didn't say anything about coming back," he says, "but she had a suitcase with her." The kid waits for my response, but I can't find words. I'll have to call her, but if she is upset enough to leave, I am pretty sure I'll get her voicemail, which starts out with her prim voice saying, "Jesus saves." And now an unwelcome flash of memory. I woke briefly, saw Auntie through my half-lidded eyes. She was standing in front of me, crying. And then I went back under.

The kid is almost to the front door when I come to my senses. "Wait," I call. The door has not closed. "Could you come back in a couple of hours?"

The kid doesn't return to the room. "I have to ask my mom, but sure," he says. "For how much?"

Every Good Samaritan Has His Price

Waited. Can't call Gloree or Auntie, and I'm not in the mood to explain to anyone how it came to be that I am trapped in a chair with a watercolor Pekingese as my only companion. My one act of normalcy was to call the woman who'd paid me to record her pet for the ages. Maybe in the back of my head I hoped she'd be so excited that she'd come over and help me to the bathroom. But like a lot of people, she is done dealing with me in person and just wants me to ship it. Right about now I'd forego her payment for that trip across the house. Instead, I make do with the glass that got me into this mess in the first place, relieving myself to its brim, pouring that out the window, and going for it one more time. I make a mental note to never, ever drink out of that glass again.

I'm the last stop on the physical therapist's schedule so I'm not desperate enough yet to call someone and ask for help. And I have the neighbor kid as a backup. Auntie may have abandoned me for good reason, but I'm not about to reveal myself as some desperate creature full of remorse and apology. Largely because I'm not, anyway.

Outside, the sun is low in the sky, maybe an hour or so away from sunset. I don't recall ever seeing the light hit the artichoke fields quite this way, each plant backlit in silvery white, as if illuminated by a jagged aura. The rows are broken up by leaf shadow, but still manage to assert a linear component so that the plants themselves look like some sort of alien marching band waiting for the parade to start. I pick up my sketchbook and rough out the scene.

I haven't done a spontaneous sketch like this in a long time and it's clear I'm rusty. Flipping through the first half of that book I see golden retrievers, terriers, and lots of mutts, but not a single sketch that isn't attributable to a photo.

I take two stabs at it. The first comes out as if I'm drawing a field of flames. I feel like I should put a smiley face on the sun and add some of those curved V's children use to represent flying birds. But the second one is better, the rows and plants come through, though I haven't captured the light correctly. It doesn't work in graphite, but if I ever paint a scene like that I'm sure I can make it work.

As I finish the last sketch, Gloree calls. "Thanks," she begins cheerily. "Mrs. Apton says you guys hit it off."

"Mrs. Apton?" I ask, breaking a cardinal rule of the chronically blacked out. Assume all unfamiliar names are people you've met. And just as quickly as I respond, I have a vague flash. A woman called right before I went under. Throaty voice.

"My client."

"Right," I say. "I've been so caught up in finishing this damn Pekingese, I can't keep my head straight. Just did a little sketching of the artichoke fields too." I add the last part because I know Gloree will want to hear that I'm serious about the art. I don't add that Auntie hired a ten-year-old kid to babysit me until I came out of my stupor.

"She says you're quite funny and that you seem to know exactly what kind of painting she wants above the fireplace."

I am the funny inebriate, I've been told. So it's always a relief to find out I was the life of the party. The Pekingese mocks me from the canvas, its grotesque little mouth smirking like this is a come-uppance for expressing on a daily basis how ugly it is. “About that, Gloree,” I say, trying to cover. “Mrs. Apton seems hard to please. I’m thinking another painter might make her happier.”

“No, no, no, Tommy. She loves you. Don’t let me down. This could be a big deal for both of us.” Some women might offer up their pouty voice but Gloree has a firm manner that generally wins me over. Ben, too, was persuasive this way.

After we hang up I look again at my sketches. The reminder that I can draw something other than dogs startles me. Not that they are remarkable. My lines aren’t as sure as they should be, but there’s definitely a kinetic quality. And more than that, it’s the first piece in a long time that I might actually care to show anyone. Except, of course, the house is empty and it has never sounded more so.

How long will Auntie remain angry with me? After my parents’ funeral it took six months before we spoke again. The services were at her church, a high-ceilinged, yellow-windowed place Pops never would’ve set foot in. A bright-blue carpet ran down the center aisle, pooling at the front beneath a lectern, dozens of flower arrangements, and my parents’ open caskets. The pews were filled with darkly dressed men and women. I’d been to several funerals with my mother where she made it a point to dress formally, but brightly, at least by comparison. “I don’t want to add to the sadness,” she told me once.

I was supposed to take my place next to Auntie and Marie,

Pops's cousin that he thought of like a sister. But I couldn't do it, couldn't sit up there in front of everyone. Auntie and I entered the foyer of the church with its permanent donation box and bulletin board of neatly pinned announcements. I saw the caskets through the open double doors. The portrait I'd painted sat between them. Looking at Auntie I asked, "Whose idea was that?"

Auntie was weepy eyed and barely holding it together. She wore her dark funeral dress with a simple mother-of-pearl brooch, and her shiny black purse was crammed with tissues she was already well into. "What are you asking me, dear?" She looked genuinely confused, so I pointed at the portrait.

"I sent it over last night," Auntie said.

I was so out of it I didn't notice the painting had been taken off the wall at home. "You should have asked me," I said sternly. "You should have asked."

Auntie was clearly shaken by my tone, and she began to sob loudly. Everyone in the church turned and looked at us. Marie rushed from the front to Auntie's side. She didn't ask why Auntie was crying, and why would she under the circumstances? Instead, she put her arm around Auntie and quietly ushered her to the front. But I didn't follow. I could barely get past the entryway to the church. So I sat in the rear corner in a row of people I'd never met, and given the fact they never once looked at me, it's possible they didn't even know who I was. Years later Auntie told me that Marie wanted to come get me but Auntie told her not to.

After the service, Auntie and Marie exited first and the pews emptied out. Whether people looked at me as they left I don't know. I kept my head down until the front half of the church was clear. The plan was for a family graveside service, but I didn't go out to our limousine. Instead, I took a breath and walked to the front where my parents' caskets rested, now closed. I picked up their portrait and took a side door to the parking lot where one of my father's surprised friends agreed to give me a ride home. Auntie checked on me through my parents' attorney, but she didn't come to the house and didn't call. I didn't want her to.

All these years later the shoe is on the other foot. I sit in a chair, sketches in hand hoping that she'll walk through the door. I want the phone to ring and for it to be Auntie, because I can't call her.

If I could see myself now as a fly on the wall it would be a pretty miserable sight, a middle-aged, hobbled painter of dogs, sitting at a window with failing light. The physical therapist never arrives, never calls. The thought comes to me that somehow Auntie canceled the appointment. But she is more direct than that—I hope. Suddenly I'm counting on her Christian heart.

The person who does step into the house is the neighbor kid. It is pretty dim, but I see him leaning into the doorway of my room, arms crossed, looking like an irritated father waiting for an explanation. "You're still sitting there?"

"I like the view," I tell the little smart-ass, a name I purposely don't blurt because I need him. I've winnowed down the best uses of his time in distinct order: (1) get alcohol from garage, (2) help me to the restroom, and (3) help me back to the bed. Even though he's a kid, he's a sturdy little thing, fat, yes, but the kind of bulldoggy fat some kids grow out of. I have taken a similar route, his size when I was young, then thin, and now plumping out around the middle as I've gotten older.

"So," the kid says, "where's my money?"

"You haven't done anything."

He stands up straight and shakes his head. "You haven't paid me yet."

It seems like everyone around me feels entitled to challenge me, and in my own home. "I can't exactly pay you if I don't get some help out of this chair," I say.

The kid flips on the light. He really is a barrel of a boy, but he's cleaned himself up since earlier in the day. He wears a white T-shirt, and his hair is sharply parted and wetted back. It's the kind of look my mother used to make me take on, at a minimum, when we went shopping. I explain how we might get me up, how I don't have any push from my legs, and where he'll have to shove and steady.

The kid stands next to me, listening to my directions, nodding his head as if to say, "Of course, how else?"

"What would you do," he says, "if I didn't show up?"

"Sit here, I guess," I say.

"Forever?"

"Well, eventually I'd have to make some calls."

The kid stares at the painting of the Pekingese, turning to me with a wrinkled nose. Just what I need, a punk and an art critic. "Did you try standing up on your own yet?"

"It's too early."

"How do you know that if you haven't tried?" He sounds incredulous, like a coach on the verge of cutting me from the team.

We are acting out a scene from *Heidi*, my ill-tempered wheelchair-bound girl to his Shirley Temple, only without her cheeriness. Or he is my Chinese Hayley Mills with no ability or intention of lifting my spirits. "I'm not looking for a Pollyanna," I say. "Just a little help to my feet."

It isn't easy, and it hurts, but eventually I rise into a standing position. The kid is strong. He stands back from me and the walker and gestures toward the doorway. Upright, I reprioritize. Bathroom first. Booze second. The kid doesn't realize it, but he is witnessing history.

The walk down the hallway is long and slow. With the kid at my side I feel very old. When I was about his age we'd gotten a visit from one of Pops's older relatives, Great-Uncle Dan. He was a tall, spindly old thing who used two canes when he walked, which kind of gave him the slope and gait of a giraffe. Every time he got up someone had to walk alongside. That job fell to me a couple of times and I remember thinking how pitiful Great-Uncle Dan was and what a pain in the ass. And years later here I am just as helpless, with a kid walking behind me probably thinking the same thing or worse.

And then of course I confirm my lameness by asking the question adults fall back on when they have nothing to say to a child and they think they're being funny. "So," I ask, "got a girlfriend?"

"I like boys," the kid says.

I stop walking. "What?"

"I like boys," he repeats.

I nod and restart our snail's-pace progress. "Oh," I say. "Are you serious?"

"Yep." The certainty in his voice is startling. I look down at him searching for a hint of a smile or maybe a wink. All I get is the sternness of his neatly parted hair.

"How can you possibly know that at your age?"

He shrugs. "Just do."

We arrive at the bathroom door. "Well," I say, "be careful," though I have no idea what danger I am warning him against. But that's what we say to boys who aren't straight, as if there's some uniquely awful person lurking just around the corner . . . another boy who is after one thing. It's the same way people warn their daughters. But that's not really on my mind. I'm more interested in getting the kid to hunt around the garage for my banished friends.

When I tell him which bottles to look for, he narrows his eyes. "Isn't that what got you into trouble?"

"Yeah, kid," I say. "It's what always gets me into trouble. But help me out anyway."

He's off to the garage and I take the last steps into the bathroom myself, the walker framing my waist. My reflection in the mirror may as well be in a fun house. I am a mess, hair cowlicked on one side, two streaks of paint on my right cheek, unshaven and reddish as if

I've been out for a jog. This was Auntie's last look at me, and the kid's first. Even on my worst benders I rarely end up in such bad shape. And though I take more after Mom than Pops, it's his face that is staring back at me. His face from one morning when I was fifteen.

Mom and Auntie were in Chicago, which Pops took as his cue to spend practically the entire weekend at the Cock's Comb, a bar not too far from the house. The first night he got home around 12:30, fairly early for him. I'd fallen asleep on the couch and he shook me awake. He was drunk, but not gone. He'd walked home. Pops was the kind of drinker that could look most people straight in the eye and talk a streak and they'd never know he was three sheets to the wind. But Mom and I could always tell, and that night he was fine, a little messy, maybe, mustard rubbed into his shirt, but otherwise pretty straight. He poured himself vodka on the rocks, all the while telling me how great the guys were down at the bar. "I wish your mother got along with them better," he said. He sat down across from me and complained about marriage until he finished his drink. Then he laughed, as if he realized I wasn't one of the guys down at the bar who could chip in with nagging-wife stories. He got quiet and looked at the television. It was showing a wide-open loft apartment with large unframed paintings leaning against the wall. A young redheaded woman who was supposed to be the artist was taking off her clothes in front of a man in a black suit. "You go for that kind of girl?" Pops asked, kicking off his shoes.

"Sure," I say, winking. "But not on a first date."

Pops nodded and smiled. He stood and poured himself another

drink. "You know what, boy? I see you all cramped up in that room of yours with your painting shit. You know what? I'm going to build you a studio."

"Wow, Pops," I said. "That'd be great." And I knew it would happen if I reminded him. I thanked him and told him I was tired. Pops must have had a couple more drinks after I went to bed because sometime during the night he got it into his head to go back to the bar and get his car. Early in the morning, I woke up feeling uneasy. I figured I'd find Pops passed out in the living room, but nothing. It was just before sunrise. I looked out the window to see the car parked halfway in the daylilies that bordered the driveway. And Pops was still in it, sleeping upright, one leg out of the open door, as if he'd conked out mid-exit. I went to get him, hoping for Mom's sake none of the neighbors had seen him.

Pops was shoeless. He'd walked all the way to the bar without shoes, leaving his white socks dark and wet. Nobody noticed? His head was kind of cocked back and he was breathing with a half snore. I touched his shoulder. He was boiling hot, his body burning off all that alcohol I guessed. "Pops," I said, shaking him lightly. He roused slowly, his head turning unsteadily in my direction. He was half lidded, stubbly, the back of his head sporting his version of a graying cock's tail. I'd seen the aftermath of his drinking a number of times, but never quite like this. It was hard to see this wreck of a man as my father. I got him to bed and for a second I thought of washing his clothes so Mom wouldn't find out. But then, there were the crushed daylilies, so what was the point?

The kid knocks on the bathroom door. I've taken a long time to get myself together, part of it just trying to disconnect how I felt about Pops being passed out in the car. A wet towel and the once-over with the electric razor are a pathetic start, but veneer will have to do. "I got to go," the kid says, knocking. I take a breath, get a good grip on the walker, and ask him to open the door.

I don't know what I'm expecting, maybe his wide-eyed amazement that the man who entered the bathroom is not the same man coming out. But he just stands there, looking at me, frustrated, two brown bags at his side. "Where do you want these?" he asks.

I lean forward. He's brought in mostly clear stuff. I want to tell him to set it all on my bed and lock the door behind him. But instead I tell him where the bar is in the living room. I have too much to figure out. Even though my legs are killing me, I've found a sense of balance and so I get slowly, painfully, down the hall without the kid behind me, though he makes two trips with the booze and then some by the time I make it to the front door to see him out. He looks at me but doesn't make a move to leave and it takes me a while to catch on. He is waiting to get paid. I tell him where he can find my wallet, which sends him running into the bedroom.

After we settle up, he turns to leave. It's a transaction based on service, after all, and he is, essentially, a stranger. But I feel odd just parting. "What's your name, kid?" I ask.

He remains facing the door, his T-shirt pinched on either side by a roll of fat. He pauses, turns, and looks me straight in the eyes, and in a flash I see it. He's handsome and confident. Fat is not a liability. It's fullness and confidence. "I'm fine with Kid," he says. With that, he leaves. It's dark outside and the house, though lit, feels dark inside as well. There's a pain pill in my room, which is where I'm headed, inch by excruciating inch, all the way thinking about what do to about Auntie and Gloree's client, what to do about Gloree, who, at that moment, is the person I want to see most.

32 Down

"Phial." That's the first word Gloree ever spoke to me. She was standing above me on the bus because I'm one of those guys who never thinks to give up his seat to a woman. And after all those years I barely recognized Ben in Gloree. I was doing a crossword puzzle, which is not my thing, so it was slow going. Gloree saw me run my pen under the clue about a million times and I guess she couldn't stand it any longer. I looked up, surprised that I hadn't seen her there all along. She was blonde then, one side cut long, the other sheared. A leopard-skin pocketbook with a bike-chain handle dangled from her hand. She stood out, for sure, but then again, I wasn't really watching for women. The last two had given me the heave-ho. Jenny, in fact, broke up with me twice in twenty-four hours. The second time because I'd been so drunk the night before I didn't remember that she told me it was over.

"I'm sorry, Tommy," Gloree said, smiling. "I just couldn't watch you suffer anymore." It was Bennie. Ben!

She'd solved *Middle English for a small closed or closeable vessel* upside down. "Oh," I said, catching on, "vial." The puzzle was called "Etymology." "I'm not that good."

"From the looks of all those empty squares, I'd agree."

I liked her directness, and I guess she went for my helplessness. In a half hour we were sitting at SereniTea, which was a fairly new place I'd never been because, well, it was tea. Gloree did the ordering, bringing us back a green pot and two cups. I laid the crossword puzzle between us and we went about finishing it. She did, anyway. I mostly just scratched my head and pretended to enjoy the camphor-like brew she'd chosen. But it gave us a place to start.

On the bus I'd sized her up as one of those faux-arty women who had a sense of personal style but probably couldn't back it up. But she was my Ben come back, so I said yes to tea. And there I was finding out she *could* more than back it up. "*This* is what I do," she said, extending her arm to the room. In its day, the building had been an auto-repair garage. Now it was all sandblasted brick and dark-brown human-sized ceramic jars. In the center were two wide tables that Gloree called altars where they sold incense and candles, and neatly packaged parcels of loose-leaf tea. We were sitting by the most startling feature, a koi pond accented by potted bamboo beneath a massive skylight crosshatched with chicken wire. Gloree told me she was the designer.

When she asked me what I did, I shied. Dog portraiture couldn't compare, so I told her I was an artist, which was true, though it had been a few years since I painted anything I could honestly call art."What medium?" she asked, leaning back in her chair and bringing her hand to her chin as if she was positioning herself to pass judgment on my response.

"Canine," I said, laughing, knowing only I got the joke. "I'm a painter. Oil and watercolor."

She took a sip of her tea and nodded. "I'm glad we met, Tom," she said, leaning forward. Her eyes were impossibly green, and in that incarnation, her lashes were curled and extra black.

"Me too," I said. "It's been a while." We talked for a long time, long enough for more tea, and for the skylight to shift from blue to lavender. Maybe the most endearing thing about her toward the end of that first time together was that she got kind of sad. She talked about feeling guilty at this little sliver of happiness we were sharing. The city had gone through an awful streak of murders, thirty-two people in less than three weeks. And it wasn't in the usual places, either. A seventy-four-year-old woman suffocated her two grandchildren in Hancock Park. A Chinese businessman and his wife were shot and dumped in the Los Angeles River, their shoes missing, but not the wallet or purse. We'd had a stretch of unrelenting heat, which seemed to set the whole city on edge. "It doesn't seem fair," Gloree said, "that the two of us can casually have tea while the rest of LA is going crazy."

"Would it make you happy," I asked, "if someone came in right now and shot us both?"

"Just me," she says, patting my hand. "I'm expendable, but the world needs art."

This all seemed so promising, this chance meeting that didn't want to end. I had a card on me but I wasn't quite ready to explain dog portraiture. So I wrote my number on our credit card receipt.

"You know, I still have your painting at my mom's house."

"But you ditched the play pants."

"No," she said firmly, sitting up. "I've embraced my options."

I felt stupid as hell and not so confident that I hadn't changed much over the years. Mostly, though, I was conflicted. One minute here was this person I'd just reconnected with whom I could so easily fall for, and the next minute, well, that's the thing, she was still a person I could easily fall for, but she was Ben. Maybe if we'd been drinking boilermakers instead of tea I might have popped off with something stupid. But I was in control and we actually talked. She told me about how when I knew her as Benita she felt like something was wrong, like she was living a half-filled life. She knew she was bisexual. She spoke about how even as a kid she hardly ever spent a dime. She put everything in savings because she knew all along where her life was headed, and she was going to afford the freedom. Even now, she was sometimes Ben the playground defender from back when, and sometimes she was Gloree, her adopted legal name.

It wasn't noble of me or anything, stupid and awkward as hell, to be honest, but none of her story seemed all that dramatic. I listened to Gloree and she seemed happy, seemed more distressed over all the murders in LA than any detail of her own life. And to be truthful, I was perhaps even a little bit envious because there was no way I could have talked about my own life with such confidence.

"Well, then," she said, clearly tired of talking about herself. "When can I see your paintings?"

Gloree's Whole

I had work to do. Shortly after we reconnected, Gloree was coming over the next evening to take a look at my attic studio. I was nervous, for sure, about her visit, and suddenly, about her, not about her, about me. I wasn't good enough. But she was coming over, it was set, and in spite of all of my confusion, every doubt was punctuated with the big fat reality that I wanted to see her.

If Gloree had seen the studio that first day we met, she would have found a half-finished oil of a Boston terrier sitting on the steps of a brownstone apartment. Leaning against the wall was a large canvas of a Cavalier King Charles and a smaller watercolor of a red-eyed basset hound. I doubted that this was the art Gloree thought the world needed. So I pulled out some of my older canvases, the landscapes, an abstract of the fiberglass mammoths at the La Brea Tar Pits, and a portrait of a former girlfriend, which was a complete rip-off of Wyeth, but a good one.

And then the canvas I put on the easel, not because it was particularly strong, but because it was different, and also unfinished. I had to have something that looked like I was working. In his book on the life of the average artist, Brolin Marx writes that as long as you're *thinking* about it, "it's in progress." So, on my easel, my painting went from aborted to resuscitated without a single brushstroke.

I stood back and looked at what was mostly pencil sketches on canvas. A couple of years earlier I'd been to a mall where they'd installed a full-size carousel, unhappy-looking horses impaled on brass poles bobbing up and down to demented calliope music. There were three or four couples standing in line to take their young children for a ride, each of them smiling and pointing in anticipation. That night I went home and made some sketches. My carousel was to be themed around the River Styx, black lit, skeletal, demons rather than ponies. I only got the painting itself partially complete before I lost momentum. What was I channeling, a high school heavy metal rebel?

But still, for Gloree, I thought maybe it would give me an edge in her arty eyes. I figured out a whole narrative, too, on why it was clearly not recent. I'd tell her about the dog-portraiture gigs, how they paid the bills, but that what I was actually about was "real" art. The kind that wasn't for a paycheck. Of course, I never even thought about the fact I was beginning our relationship on a false premise, that Gloree would believe me and think of me as an artist. That I'd have to actually finish that painting, and a number of others just to keep up the fiction. I call it my no-clue period.

Another thing. Gloree met me at the worst time possible because I was just a couple of days into big-time antibiotics for a "boggy prostate," as the doctor called it. No alcohol for a couple of weeks. Nothing. Cold turkey, which for me meant a couple of glasses of wine here and there but that's it. Mostly. A shot of bourbon when I was setting up the studio for Gloree. And a beer, which I didn't even enjoy, when I ran into an old friend at the art store. So Gloree was getting me flat-out sober, my version of, which maybe was not so good.

On the alcohol count, Los Angeles's misfortune saved my butt. When Gloree arrived at my door, she looked distressed, though beautiful still, and I didn't think about Ben at all. No. I did. I had such a crush. Now I had a second chance, only with the woman who had taken me to tea and helped me with a crossword puzzle.

"Tom," she said, striding into the room and plopping down on the couch as freely as if she'd done it a million times before. She wore a strapless lime-green dress that hugged her frame tightly, an odd spray of gathers at each hipbone, like the grasped hands of an invisible child afraid to let go of its mother. I had chosen a smart green linen jacket with off-white slacks. We could have been part of a wedding party. "There's been another one. They found a woman shot in the Hollywood Green." That made thirty-three in a little over two weeks. The Green was the nature corridor they'd opened up through Hollywood. Whoever killed the woman dumped her over the fence, which wasn't altogether uncommon. Coyotes and other scavengers were known to be fairly uncomplicated tools to eliminate forensic evidence. Gloree described how the woman's corpse had been disemboweled, her eyes missing as well as all her fingers and toes. Early-morning joggers pounded on the fence to scare the coyotes away.

In the old days, before the corridors, we liked the fact that skunks and possums wandered the city at night raiding our garbage cans. And we didn't care all that much when we heard about a yappy dog being snatched out of its yard by one of the coyotes. The presence of these animals wandering our urban landscape made us feel like we hadn't gone entirely wrong.

I broke out the wine. Gloree drank three glasses to my one, all the while extending her lament. I tried to get her off the topic, not because I didn't care, but because she did seem to be taking it all so personally, as if each and every victim were a family member. But no matter what I brought up she always came back to the murders, talking about each person as if they were thirty-three coffins right there with us, each open and ready for viewing, as if she were responsible.

"Look," I finally said, "none of this belongs on your shoulders."

She shook her head. "Right. It belongs on all of ours."

I asked if she'd ever read Glenella Dolmer's *Parsing Peace.* It's a slim little thing, but it's dead on about the role of the individual in creating a stable society. She says that "extended focus and the evil acts of a few obscure the fact that many thousands of acts of goodness are performed each day and go unreported and unnoticed. The individual who doesn't recognize these, who embraces mourning, exacts a greater toll on society than any despot could possibly hope for."

"I guess I'm aiding and abetting."

I offered a shrug and nod to let her know that I agreed, and in that moment Gloree became more to me than all confidence and energy. Right then she was also pure heart and worry, complete. I fell in love at that moment and never looked back. Ben and Thomas and Gloree.

The Road to Gloree

Ben left our school in the middle of seventh grade. Puberty hit her fast and hard, and when we took showers after gym, she told me, it was pretty noticeable. The rest of her class was still hairless, round as cherubs, and sporting unimpressive nubbins, while she was fully nested. Her locker was next to mine, and one day after gym she pulled out a small box. "Look what Mom and Dad gave me last night." It was a box of condoms, though, to be honest, I wasn't quite sure what that gesture meant. Sex education had not been a strong suit of Mr. Paul, our science teacher. Ben could tell I was confused.

"The guy slips them over his dick so you don't get chicks pregnant." She pulled one out. It wasn't rolled into a small square package, but rather hung between her fingers, dry and hazy white like a snakeskin tied off at one end.

"Gross," I said. But what I was thinking was I couldn't imagine how long, if ever, I'd be able to fit into something that big. And honestly, it suddenly made me think about undressing for the shower after PE. How could I drop my underwear if I was supposed to fit into a deflated dirigible?

"Yep. They told me to bring them to wherever I take my boyfriends." She cupped her breasts in mock pride.

I was surprised that Ben had never mentioned this hidden man harem. "You have boyfriends?"

She was reaching into the locker, but paused and looked at me as if I was the biggest idiot she'd ever met. "No. Don't want any."

"Then what's the deal?"

"The deal is," Ben said, lowering her voice to keep anyone in the hallway from hearing, "I just haven't been spending a lot of extra time at home is all."

She hadn't been spending much time with me either, I thought. Though I know why now. Precisely when everyone was telling her she was becoming a woman, her body and mind was encouraging all her options. And all that time away from home wasn't spent with boys. She was practical. She went to the library to search through human sexuality reference books. The librarians assumed she was thinking about becoming a doctor someday. When she didn't get the answers she wanted, partly because she didn't know what she was looking for, she tried making an appointment with a psychiatrist, who refused (1) on grounds that her parents didn't know, and (2) Ben didn't have any money.

Ben was forced to do what she tells me a lot of kids do . . . suck it up until you can get away. She reinvented, and not that it's a consolation all these years later, but she's dating a nice woman I've never been introduced to. Shanna.

Doing Lines

It's only been a few days since Auntie left and I'm making a list of all my awful qualities. The worst thing is to be an artist who makes promises. I'll meet this or that deadline. Sure, I'll have that done by Wednesday at the latest. Because, no matter what, we won't begin until Tuesday night. But I am in a predicament with Gloree because my promise to her feels almost like an unspoken last straw. Maybe she doesn't even know it herself, but if I don't have a painting for her client in a couple of weeks, I'm certain I'll be out of her life for good, and this time for good for good.

Now I'm back in bed and have a blank canvas staring at me, the blankest canvas I've ever seen. My consolation is that I'm still in bed, and so, at least, the whiteness is more like the distant light of a train coming down the tracks than an engulfing blizzard. At least there is the comfort of knowing that I can jump off the rails even at the last second. Though this time I am determined to do some locomotive wrestling, an easy kind of determination to have when all my paints are well out of reach.

I have no idea what Gloree's client wants and no way to contact her. Not taking calls during her cruise, the message says. "Mailbox is full." "Mailbox is full." "Mailbox is full." It's a large canvas. Somewhere in storage I have an abstract whippet a client never picked up. Or, could I rip off Pollock, maybe Barnett Newman? Just pay Kid an extra few bucks to escort me to the bathroom while he comes in here and doodles around with my brushes for a while?

Kid. I'm actually looking forward to him showing up again, though that won't be for another hour or so. On the nightstand is a small notepad and a Los Angeles Zoo pencil nub sharpened short enough that the giraffe merely exists as a mini trophy head. I need to get something out and I know what it is. Kid's image is sitting in my brain, as if he's just crossed his arms and slid down the inside wall of my skull, an indifferent but persistent presence. My pencil hovers above the pad, unsure of where it wants to start and even more unsure about where it wants to end. I see Kid with that neatly combed hair, only not in the clothes he wears, but in a yellow short-sleeved shirt and plaid pants, an outfit I remember Mom buying me for our annual family photograph at the Sears photo studio. Maybe that's a look I think is better for a little gay kid. Though Vernon Delaney, who clearly had a crush on me in fourth grade, he was more of a Chuck Taylor–and-rugby-shirt kind of dresser.

But it isn't Kid's actual image I'm after. Way back in art school, one of my more challenging instructors, Ms. Cratzin, threw us a curve ball. The course was human form and we'd spent the better part of the semester with a parade of nude models, every Tuesday night new flesh, some tight, some rolling, all of it benign. And then, Ms. Cratzin brought in a different kind of model, a woman mounded to the neck in a billowy yet formless gown that seemed sewn of burlap, taffeta, and gray satin. Then, with accent I never quite figured out, Ms. Cratzin said, "Now we will see what you haf learned." With that she turned us loose, told us to ignore the material and draw only the lines of the body.

I set about this exercise with Kid, with the added challenge of not having him in front of me. The first attempts may as well be the circle drawings that make up Mickey Mouse, then maybe as a snowman, a stack of ice cream scoops, at last a boy, but too cartoony. I work at it for an hour, until, with pages running out and the pencil lead dull and thick, I strike it, the right lines, not a photocopy of Kid, but certainly his essence, because it isn't just about the outline, it's about what I see inside him, not outside, as if shadows are his bones.

I hear the front door open. Kid.

Flipping through the pad, it becomes a kind of animation of metamorphosis, beach ball to boy in two seconds. I looked up and Kid is standing in the doorway, stern and in a tight green sweatshirt, not the boy in my drawing but exactly him at the same time. Not a kid who looks anything like the friends I had growing up. Even in high school I couldn't have drawn a Chinese kid from memory. Were there no Chinese families in our neighborhood? "What are you doing?" Kid asks.

I'm caught off guard not by his question, but because the answer comes to mind immediately and in a form I haven't used in a long time. "I'm *doing* art."

i, kid: intervention i—i—i

Starry, Starry Blight

Kid got me to the bathroom and perched in front of my easel and now I'm alone again. It's a big leap from small sketches to the canvas, especially when there's an expectation placed on what you're going to produce. Gloree brought me two canvases of the same size and I haven't a clue what her client needs. I think of the photographs she showed me of the woman's living room, the expanse above the fireplace that looms and mocks. The bonus bourbon Kid brought in from the garage calls, though it is in the other room. And normally it would win out, but the sketch I did of the artichoke fields catches my eye. The pad is standing vertically, so that east and west are north and south. On the left are my terrible birds, which from this angle look like scattered nail clippings. But rows of artichokes, the precise lines diminishing to a pinpoint and just as defined through a series of jagged forms, make for an interesting effect. I turn the canvas on the easel in the same position as the pad and pick up a pencil. I have no idea if it can work on a larger field, but at least I'm interested in finding out. And then, of course, there are two canvases, both of them entirely white, as if space has been overtaken entirely by stars, or perhaps it's the bright light reported in near-death experiences. Either way, it is my job to bring back the dark.

No paint on the canvas yet, but I'm well into sketching out a direction when Kid catches me off guard by appearing at my bedroom door. I'm beginning to wonder if he has any clothes that fit, this time his pants ride high around the ankles and the sleeves of a gray sweatshirt stop well short of his wrists. "Hey," he says with a tone of surprise, "you're not drunk."

I put down my pencil. "Imagine that."

"You still need me?"

"How are you at bartending?" He doesn't laugh. Need him? He is what, ten or eleven? I'm a grown man and I've managed to muddle through life without an assistant. Right now is just a little rough patch. That is what Auntie was supposed to be for, to shepherd me through the injuries until I was literally back on my feet. Only, the shepherd has abandoned her flock.

"Yes," I say. "I could use your help."

Kid brightens and walks through the room to the window next

to me. "I thought it was pretty creepy the way you were watching me that one time."

"People look out of windows."

"Yeah, but you weren't looking. You were studying."

"Hey," I say, pointing to the canvas. He stands next to me smelling kind of like Pops's after-shave. I reorient the canvas so that it's clear what I've been drawing. "See. Just field. No Kid."

He shrugs. "I should be in it," he says, pointing to the edge of my version of the field. "That part right there is because I water."

It is probably true. He belongs in the painting as much as the artichokes, but it wouldn't make sense once I turn the piece back on its side. And besides, there is a larger problem. "I don't paint people," I tell him. I haven't done a worthwhile painting with a human in it since my parents died, since I saw my portrait of them at their memorial service.

Kid seems nonplussed. He sits on my bed. "I never met anyone with as many problems as you."

"Did you come over to help me or harass me?"

"I came over to see if you needed anything, and to ask for a favor."

I turn the wheelchair around to face him. "What's that?"

"I found a box of stuff when we moved. A green box. I think it was my father's and I need a place to see what's in it."

"Why don't you just ask your father?"

"He's dead."

I'm confused. I've seen his mother roll his father up their wheelchair ramp. "Who," I ask, "is the disabled man living with you now?"

"My brother." He scratches behind his ear waiting for my next question. This is a mindblower because I'd already thought the man that his mother pushed in the wheelchair was way too old for her, she with the long, shiny black hair cut flat across right above her waist, he, Kid's brother, semijowled and white-haired at the temples, stoic.

"I take it," I finally say, "your father was very old?"

"I guess," he says, incredulous. "But my brother is also very sick, and still less trouble than you." He squints his eyes as if to dare me to challenge him.

I look at the painting. *If I did add him to it*, I think, *he'd be a dark pulsing smudge at the edge of the field.* Too tough for his age he is, but I like him. "Sure," I say, "bring over whatever you got. The living room is all yours."

He hops off the bed. "Need a drink?"

Kid cuts me off at two vodkas so I actually get some work done. Actually, he sits on the bed watching me paint and I shake my glass for a third. "No," he says.

From Auntie I had to take no, but I am paying him. "Seriously, I'm good, get me another."

"No." It is midafternoon and we've drawn the curtains slightly to keep the light even. His eyes are two thin, determined corridors of black. "Two is enough." He slides off the bed and takes my glass. It seems like I've won, but he sets the glass down on the floor and walks back to the window, peering out briefly. "Come here," he says. I set down my brush and extract my legs from beneath the easel, still getting the hang of maneuvering the chair. Kid isn't any help, just watches while I make a fifteen-point turn to get to him. What am I paying him for?

At the window, we look down on his porch where the old man who is his brother sits in a wheelchair as well. He holds a cigarette, dangling it over the edge of the banister, thread-like smoke wisping in the breeze. He never actually brings the cigarette to his mouth, just stares stiffly forward. "I thought you said it was creepy to look at people from the window," I say to Kid.

"I said *you* were creepy."

"He ever actually smoke that thing?"

Kid looks at me. We are eye to eye, he in all his plump intensity, surprisingly formidable. "He'd like to, but he can't raise his arms. But he says that's how he's always done his thinking, while smoking, so now Mom lights his cigarette and lets him think."

It's a rough story, but I'm not sure exactly why Kid let me in on it. From our vantage, it seems as if his cigarette has burned pretty well down to the nub. "What happens," I ask, "when the cigarette goes out?"

"Sometimes it burns his fingers. In our old house there were about a million brown holes in our kitchen floor."

I focus again on Kid's brother, who hasn't moved at all, a kind of Chinese Abraham Lincoln on the Mall. This man wears almost all white from jacket to pants, brown socks and shoes. His hair is stacked tall but pomaded back. "What happened to him?"

Leaning on my window in a gesture of confidence, as if this is precisely the question he's been waiting for, Kid offers his version of a knowing smile, no real broadening, but the slightest separation of lip, revealing that indeed he does have teeth.

"Charles was a cock fighter."

"That's not legal."

I don't have permission to speak, Kid shaking his head just enough to let me know this. "He was a cock fighter for a long time but he started to get sick of it. So then other people fought his roosters for him. That meant he didn't have to keep his head straight so he started drinking, mostly tequila. This is all before he came to live with Mom and me. I wouldn't even have known I *had* a brother except he ran his car into the corner of someone's house. The first time I met him was at the hospital."

Kid looks at me to see if I get it. I do. Auntie has clearly died and reincarnated in record time. "It's nice of you," I say, and I mean it, "but that's not my future."

"You're right, it's not," he says, looking me up and down. "It's you right now."

Jesus Saves

A solid week goes by and the physical therapist has convinced me I am better off using the walker than the chair as long as at first I have Kid rolling it behind me just in case. Still no Auntie, and I know better than to call. Besides, I am trying Kid's new two-drink program, which worked great for six days. But on the seventh day, I rested . . . a lot.

The man at the door has a scruffy beard, is bright-eyed and brown skinned, not so much brown, I guess, as maybe tea colored, and it is skin with depth, layers, the translucence and substance of handblown glass. He spends a lot of time in the sun. Then again, that might all be because I installed one of those yellow bug lights, which, right then, in the late-evening dark, is hosting a party of moths despite its purpose. "Sorry I'm so late," the man says, smiling. "I'm Jesus." And again he doesn't pronounce it the Spanish way, but more like Geezus, as in "of Nazareth." And it comes out thin and pure, like milk through cheesecloth.

"Yes," I say. "Late. My aunt has been gone for a while." I'm a bit snockered, and doing the unwise thing of using my walker without any backup. We stand at the door for a moment and he never stops smiling, army surplus from head to foot, olive green down to an overstuffed duffel bag cradled between his combat boots. Behind him, the yellow light fades into the mostly dark neighborhood, a few lights in the distance winking from behind eucalyptus, the artichoke fields a diminishing ethereal glow. Finally, Jesus raises his eyebrows in a request to be let in. I have bourbon killing ice in the living room and if I promised this guy something, a promise is a promise, though I need to keep my guard up.

I follow, the walker now a kind of extension of myself, as if I am a six-legged animal running in slow motion. There is nothing graceful about my new guest, boots clomping across the wood floor, duffel snatching the yin-yang throw rug as he drags it behind him.

"Drink?" I ask.

"Rarely touch it," he says. "A little wine now and then." He plops himself on the couch and looks around the room, alighting on a photograph of my mother and father in their burnt-orange-and-avocado-green phase, Pops wearing the same "dress-up" tie he took out for every wedding, funeral, and church potluck. "Parents?" Jesus asks. "I don't have any photos of mine."

"Right," I say, looking at his duffel. I sit and take a swig of bourbon, not knowing what to say, and so I go straight to my worst option. "To tell you the truth," I offer, "I can't remember exactly why you're here."

Jesus laughs and shakes a finger at me, in the playful way of a happy old man. Like a knowing rabbi, maybe. "I thought you'd say that," he mocks. "You were pretty smashed."

I raise my glass to him and take a drink, letting an ice cube into my mouth for the clarity of coldness on my tongue. "Wouldn't be the first time."

"Sounds like kind of a problem," Jesus says, taking off his boots, a gesture that I immediately take as permanence.

"Only," I say, "if people expect one to remember conversations. And ninety-nine percent of human interaction is bullshit, so the odds against missing something important are with me." I toast again and empty my glass. I want another, but I'm with it enough to hold off. With it enough to be suspicious that maybe a few more and I'll wake up and he'll be gone and so will my stereo and television and wallet, everything except Mom and Pops trapped in a frame with their Sears grins. I am desperately trying to think of where I met this guy. And what the hell, I get up—if that's what you could call the whole grimacing process I go through to stand—and pour myself another bourbon at the bar.

"Still can't remember?" Jesus is smiling again. In fact, he hasn't stopped smiling since I opened the door. "It was right here in this room at a party. A friend brought me. And your head was just about dead on center in the middle of that bar. And you distinctly said, 'Jesus help me.'"

"Very funny," I say, hobbling back to the couch. Proud that I've learned how to use the walker and transport a drink at the same time. It was Pops who taught me all kinds of bar tricks when I was a child, not only the mixing, but the delivery too. In one *Gunsmoke* commercial break I could make him a martini, double olives, balance the tumbler on my head, and walk all the way across the room to his recliner. I was so fast that Miss Kitty wouldn't get a word out before Pops had his first drink.

Jesus is staring right at me, rubbing a finger over his soul patch. "Are you saying you've never said that?"

It's getting creepy, but at the same time I'm feeling the booze so I play along. "I might have. But I meant Jesus Christ, Son of God, He who died for our sins, not Jesus Hobo, son of a bitch, he who showed up for a free meal."

Smiling, Jesus walks over to me and I visibly tense, thinking maybe he is going to hit me. "Relax, brother." He reaches out and takes my glass.

"I'm not done with that."

"Let me fix you something better." With that, he goes behind the bar and does a quick excavation peppered with mumbled "Where's the?" and "hmm"s. When he finds everything he needs, he starts mixing, the tumble of ice, bitters, bourbon, and whatever else sounding to me like a prodigal son knocking at the door. While he's doing all of this, he's also finally giving up a little history. Tells me that he manages the family business, exports. That his father is more of an idea man and isn't so good with people, so he, Jesus, takes care of all the nuts and bolts, takes the meetings with clients when it's necessary. "And right now, brother," he says, "I'm taking some time away and just tooling around. Saving a few brain cells by getting out of the day-to-day thing."

"You kind of sidestepped my main question," I say. "What are you here to help me with?"

He comes to me, drink extended, almost the same color as his skin. "I can't tell you, brother. If I did, it wouldn't be help. But I can tell you this." He tapped his wrist on a dim watchband-wide tan line. "The clock is ticking. I've got to be in Provo pretty soon."

I take the drink, suddenly unsure if maybe I am being slipped a Mickey. The room is startlingly quiet. Jesus and I are locked eye to eye as I bring the drink to my lips. It smells like overripe oranges, fruit fallen from a tree, still good, but turning. "Why should I trust you?" I ask.

"Leap of faith, brother, leap of faith."

Are You There God? I Need . . . Margarine?

I wake slowly, after what was clearly a deep, deep sleep. The first in a long time, since before my accident at least. Outside, the sky is just taking on its morning colors, small pink clouds assembled in popcorn-shrimp rows. And there, in the room, on the easel, the most recent version of my upturned artichoke landscape. Nothing to give Gloree, but evidence that I have indeed been using my paints. Obsession, useful as a car that can only make right-hand turns.

I rub the sleep from my eyes, thinking that today, yes today, I will call Auntie and ask for her help. I will admit that I screwed up, that I've finally made a promise I can't keep. I need her advice, her help. Gloree is expecting a painting from me and it's looking more and more like I will have nothing for her. If I had just stayed sober long enough to take her client's call I could have wiggled my way out as planned. But now, I'm about to break one of Pops's cardinal rules.

These thoughts crowd in, that and the crazy dream I had about Jesus, the guy who'd been sending me notes saying he was on his way. It seemed real, him knocking at my door, wearing fatigues, fixing me a drink. I couldn't even it make it seven days without alcohol, and it's come to this. I'm dreaming of Jesus. For some reason the monkey aviary pops into my mind.

I listen to my house carefully. Inside, nothing. Outside, a crow somewhere, taunting the oncoming day. Inside, the usual stillness. A house with one occupant, outside, the growl of the pickup that drives around the perimeter of the artichoke fields. Inside, just me, and as usual, I'm trying to remember exactly how I got into bed, trying to recall which drink put me over the edge.

I think of Pops, suddenly, because this is how it must have been for him toward the end. Mom, sleeping next to him quietly, while he rubbed his temples and got his bearings, tried to remember the previous night and any promises he may have made. And then, too, the wash of regret and apology that envelops one after a night of drinking even when the reasons aren't clear.

Those were the days of constant absolution, when Pops found himself telling me or Mom he was sorry for saying this thing or that the night before, for knocking over another vase, for denting the garage with the car, for standing in the front yard with a drink, watching neighbors who still had jobs pull into their garages—for everything. Those were our mornings at the end, queries and apologies.

The morning Mom and Pops took off for the wedding, the last time I saw them, they were running late because Pops was shaking off the night before. I remember Mom with the car door open, she in the blue knee-length dress she always wore to weddings, her fat faux pearls following a modest plunge of neckline. Pops put his arm around me, half out of affection, half out of needing to support himself. By then I was nearly as tall as him. "Your mother tells me I was a little rough on you two last night, boy."

"Not too bad," I said, fending off a conversation we'd had a half dozen times before, and too recently. Just then, he looked a little ridiculous to me, collar too tight around his neck, tie too short, the church-boy part in his hair he'd worn since, since he was a church boy.

He stood up straight and looked at me firmly. "That's not the way I heard it. Anyway, I just wanted to say I know I've been hitting it a little hard lately. I'm in kind of a rough patch with the job and all. But like I told your mother this morning, you two are the most important things in the world to me."

"Thanks, Pops," I said, quietly, meaning it, but knowing what was coming next.

"Last night was it. When we get home I told your mother we're throwing out every goddamned bottle." He patted me on the back, the other hand searching his pants pocket for keys. "What do you think about that?"

"Great," I said. We shook hands, which felt kind of silly, and I watched him and Mom drive off. As usual, she waved out the window until they were all the way around the corner. It was a goodbye I recorded even then, not because there was anything special about it, but because I told myself I didn't want either of their lives, though I loved them both. I could not be my mother, watching the person I cared for most destroy himself, could not be my father relying on his family to function as his memory. *Damage control*, I told myself, *is when you wake up, if you wake up, and the first thing you think about is what you have to fix or smooth over, and what apologies need to be made.* I would never be that way, I told myself.

Ha!

*

Toast. I smell it, and then hear it, faintly, the distinct sound of a table knife running across a crisp surface. I assume Kid must have come in, but would he have brought bread? I hear him coming down the hall, only there is something different about the sound, heavier, less urgent. Auntie? Rounding the doorway is not a boy with ill-fitting clothes nor an aunt with an ill temper. It is Jesus holding a plate of toast. Same fatigues and bushy hair, same smile. Not a drunken dream. "Morning, brother," he says. "Man, you're a handful to get to bed."

"I thought you were a dream," I say, scooting up on the head-board, suddenly tasting the rot of last night's alcohol. "What were those drinks you gave me?"

He sets the toast on my lap. "Drink. I made you *one*. You were in the driver's seat after that."

I search. Nothing. "Look," I say, "sometimes I can go a little overboard. If I got a little stupid last night, I'm sorry." And even as these last two words come out of my mouth I feel a too-tight tie and collar around my neck and a too-sharp part running through my hair.

"Don't sweat it, brother." He walks to my easel and cocks his head this way and that. "You know," he says, "you never once mentioned you were an artist."

"That's because one has to produce art in order to be an artist."

Jesus laughs and shakes his head in good-natured pity. "By the way, the kid from next door left a green box here this morning."

"Oh? What'd he say?"

Walking back toward the door, Jesus laughs again. "I believe his first words were 'Who the hell are you?'"

"That was Kid alright."

"Anyway, brother, he said he'd be back later. And I'm going to the store. Your cupboards are bare." With that he starts down the hallway.

"Hey, Jesus," I call, waiting until he pokes his head into view. "Haven't you heard about the miracle of the loaves and fishes?"

He winks. "Brother, you don't need a miracle if you've got cash."

I listen to him exit the front door. The toast remains in my lap, a little dark, but edible looking. I pick up a piece and inspect its opposite side. Not buttered. All that earlier noise was Jesus scraping off the burnt parts. It doesn't matter because I doubt that I even have any butter. In fact, I can name every single bottle restored to my liquor cabinet and honestly can't name more than five or six things in my refrigerator. I think of Jesus doing my shopping, of my blind apology to him. Clearly, I need to take inventory in more ways than one.

Clocked

It was a May wedding, cool even for that time of the year. We'd had a freak storm that swooped down from the Arctic, which soaked the entire state. Los Angeles was not spared. Clear up to Saturday morning, just hours before I waved goodbye to Mom and Pops, the sky was falling. You can love an LA sky after a storm, fat stabs of blue puncturing weakened clouds, the hum of the city converted to dampened hushing. I watched a lot of it on television, the river sluicing through the city core, rescuers tossing nets from overpasses to snatch up incautious boys, deer trapped and huddled on the concrete banks.

I sat in Pops's well-worn lounger, feet up, not interested in the book on my lap, clicking from station to station and watching my city from a half dozen news copters, none of us afraid of water, all of us defeated by it. Much of the day got away from me, 6:00 rolling around before I knew it. Mom and Pops had said they'd be back by 4:30, were just dropping by the reception to leave a gift. But by 4:31 I knew. When Pops came home, there was no way he was emptying out bottles, at least not down the drain.

Because he was who he was, and everyone there would know it, they would be putting glasses in his hand, one after the other, and he would be funny and charming and in charge. He would catch the garter, make rounds at the tables with a reel of joke toasts, none of it sounding sloppy if everyone else was drinking too. And then, a bell would ring in Mom's head—time to go—and she would discreetly grasp Pops's suggestible hand and lead him away from whatever clot of people he had gathered. At the car, there would be a brief argument, his taking umbrage at her request for keys, she, calm, experienced, knowing that there was this kernel of sobriety inside him that locked itself away in a kind of fallout shelter until the coast was clear. Then, the exchange, Pops's "Aww, what the hell," and Mom's silence. I'd seen it in action myself.

Mom didn't drive; the police told me. But before that I was watching Los Angeles fall apart as it usually does in rain, heavy or light. I thought about painting but convinced myself that the light in the studio out back would be too intermittent to be true. I was working on their portrait, a surprise for their twentieth anniversary. But as I hit the remote again and again, looking for action, always unsatisfied, I slowly came to the realization that I was alone in the house, that this was one of just a handful of times when neither of my parents was around. I was just weeks away from graduating high school, and I wondered if this is what the next few years would feel like, what being by oneself was like in a more permanent sense.

Around 9:00 when it was clear that all the "breaking news" had been reduced to recycled flood video from earlier that day, I decided to call Auntie. She'd been at the same wedding as Mom and Pops. Her phone rang. On the television, a woman in a soaked bright-pink muumuu stood on the roof of her nearly submerged car, waving frantically at her rescuer, a man in an orange suit hanging from a line thirty feet below a helicopter.

When Auntie answered, she wasn't surprised at my question

and less surprised my parents hadn't gotten home yet.

"Oh, Thomas," she began, "your father slipped and banged up his knee. He wouldn't go to the hospital."

I knew I could be direct with Auntie. "Was he drinking?"

"Of course. After he fell, your mother put him in the car and he just passed out."

The woman on the television was strapped chest to chest with her rescuer, both of them lifted toward safety. "Why didn't she just bring him home?"

"Because," Auntie sighed, "your mother put him in the driver's seat. So she just took his keys and went back to the reception. And when I left she said she was going to sit in the car and read until he came to."

I thanked Auntie and asked if she thought it was a good idea for me to drive out to wherever the reception had been. But we both decided it would embarrass Mom and upset Pops. "They're adults," Auntie reminded me, "and your mother has a lot more experience handling your father than you do."

"No," I say, "not a lot."

After we hung up, I told myself I'd give them until midnight and then I'd call the police. I turned off the television and looked around our small living room, all of it cast in the mild cream light escaping the prize crepe lampshade Mom brought home from a church bazaar. Glinting from the bookshelf was one of Pops's forgotten glasses, something Mom and I were finding more and more often. I picked it up. Bourbon, and it had to be pretty recently poured or it would have evaporated.

As I walked to the kitchen to pour it out I passed the clock. 9:12 P.M. It was going to be a long night. At the sink, I tilted the glass but stopped short of pouring out the bourbon. Even now I don't know why, because I wasn't a drinker yet, but I brought the glass to my mouth and threw the contents back, all of it in one shot, hot on my throat.

How can Pops drink this crap? I remember thinking.

I want the story to be that at 11:59 I reached for the phone and just then I heard my parents at the door. Pops would be sobered up, for him, and Mom would look relieved just to be home. She would have taken her pearl necklace off and put it in her purse, perhaps taken her shoes off just inside the door, not caring about running her stockings. "You're a sweetie for waiting up," she'd say to me. Pops would wink and rub me on the head with his big, wide hand. And in that moment, just that sliver of time, we'd be the most content family in the world.

But it's not the story I can tell. At 11:59 I was asleep, and Mom and Pops didn't come home. Pops woke up in the car after a couple of hours or so and went back to the reception, limping. The party was still going strong, everyone left was dancing and drinking, everyone except Mom who had settled into a conversation with the bride's mother. They welcomed Pops back with spontaneous cheering, half of them waving him to the dance floor, the other half waving him toward the bar. But in that one instance something had gotten hold of him. They were the Red Sea and he was Moses with an eye on the safety of a distant shore, Mom.

The bride's mother said Pops seemed perfectly fine when he walked up to her and Mom. Said he was ready to go home and even apologized for making a scene with his fall. The three of them laughed about it. Mom told the woman it was a lovely wedding and reception as she took the keys from her purse and handed them to Pops. Although I wasn't there, I know she would have done so for Pops's pride, her own public statement of confidence even if in private it was flagging.

She did let him drive, we know that. And the toxicology said he was over the legal limit, but just barely. None of that mattered. About a mile from home, a car hydroplaned through a puddle. They were broadsided, Mom killed first, Pops a second later, the car pushed into a utility pole.

People were surprised it wasn't Pops's fault, some of them expressing an odd sense of relief that it wasn't, trying to comfort me with that fact. "Freak accident" was the operational term. Of course, they were mostly trying to console themselves. I wasn't letting anyone off the hook. "No," I said more than once, "if Pops hadn't passed out they would have missed that car by two hours."

How Now Nature Cow?

I have no painting for Gloree and there is something not right, something missing about the artichoke field I did paint. I'm tired of looking at it. Done. Dog portraiture, that is what I'm good at. I hear my back door, glad that Jesus has returned. Jostling and pinging as he puts away whatever groceries he's bought. There are two voices, both hollowed out by the long hallway. After a minute or so Jesus walks into the room, Kid following him right behind holding the box he told me about.

"Brother," Jesus says, "I hope you don't mind that I let your drinking buddy in."

"I wish," I say.

Kid rolls his eyes, not interested in the adult humor, clearly with his own agenda clutched in his hands. He sits on my bed ready to go through this trunk-like box about the size of a boot, really, greenish blue, scratched. At one time it was secured with leather straps, but those were long ago broken, the ends still buckled but leading to fray.

"What exactly do you think is in there?" I ask.

This is not received as an unexpected question because Kid is quick with a reply. "We're not a very happy family," he says.

"My mother never got over my father's death. I never met him."

Kid must be the first to open the box in a long time because even from where I sit at the easel, hopelessly staring at my artichoke painting, the musty smell is distinct.

From here I see letters tied with a blue ribbon. The two of them, Jesus and Kid, are getting along as if they've known each other all their lives, Kid explaining how this box had been his father's, a man about whom his mother had told him nothing, except, when his much, much older brother came to live with them, that their father had been quite old. In fact, the box appeared with his brother with the simple statement out of his mother's earshot. "That is what is left of our father." And then Kid never saw it again.

Although I'm supposed to be paying attention to my painting, I can't help feeling a little left out, jealous of Kid and Jesus. Instead of working, I turn the television to one of the nature-cam stations. Today, there's a thin coyote standing at the fence, perhaps lamenting the precorridor days when it had free roam of the neighborhood pets.

Kid and Jesus must sense that the coyote isn't entirely holding my attention since they both look up and smile at me at the same time. I am a collector of misfits, apparently, and they beckon me to join them in exploring Kid's box. He unties the blue ribbon and holds the first piece of his puzzle, a small envelope with a hand-typed address to Mr. Catalino P. Aquino. It is stamped with a perfectly circular postmark from Manhattan, Kansas. Kid slides the letter from the neatly slit-open end. It has been folded in half and then in three sections and sits upright on the bed like a thin recliner. Kid reads it aloud.

*

January 8
Mr. Catalino P. Aquino
PO Box 877
San Luis Obispo, California

My dear Mr. Aquino:

I have received your letter of January 3 and I am glad to know that you have not given up the idea of entering this college although you are not at this time able to be here.

I am referring your transcript to the committee on admission and sometime before college opens next fall a permit to register at the beginning of the fall semester in the curriculum in agriculture will be sent to you.

I hope that it will be possible for you to be here at that time.

Very truly yours,
S. A. Nock, Vice President

Z:ML
CC- -Com.Adm.

"Cool, little brother," Jesus says. But I'm confused. Aquino is a Filipino name.

Shrugging and baffled, Kid picks up the remainder of the letters, holding them out like a hand of cards. They are a few dozen, posted from naval bases and a place I'd never heard of in California called

Highland Springs Resort. We recognize immediately that they've been kept in dated order. Kid reads each of them to us. Catalino Aquino came over from the Philippines sometime before and took jobs as a domestic servant. He had lived in Portland briefly, which we learn from a two-sentence letter of recommendation, the same letter stating that he was "a good plain cook and excellent in his housework." Not long after that he was receiving mail at the resort. Later letters from the owner there addressed from San Francisco speak admiringly of Kid's—father?—for his service to the country.

When Kid comes to an envelope that has resealed itself over the years, Jesus stops him from running his finger into it. Instead, he asks me for a letter opener. I gesture toward the nightstand. Instead of finding the opener, Jesus pulls out the pad of paper on which I made the sketches of Kid. "Well, what's this, brother?" he says as if he'd found some sort of treasure.

Kid recognizes himself immediately, even in the preliminary versions on the first pages. "I thought you said you don't paint people."

"First, those aren't paintings, and second, notice they're in the drawer and not on the walls."

"Am I really that fat?" Kid asks, placing a palm on his belly.

"No. I'm just that bad."

"Here," Kid says, pointing to one of the last drawings, "this one's good." He's right. It's small, too small to make out a true expression, but the posture is right, the attitude. That's when I know what my artichoke field is missing. I can feel the brush in my hand already.

I paint and listen as Kid and Jesus read the remaining letters, examine small black-and-white photographs used as postcards of open-casket funerals, whole Filipino families posing around the deceased—a very old woman, an infant, another infant—crude skull symbols painted on the sides of wood coffins. "Not exactly happy inspiration," I say after they interrupt my painting for the umpteenth time. But Kid has moved on to the final item, a sealed green envelope folded in four and labeled with crude block letters, *FOR EMERGENCYS*. Kid is not careful or reverent, tearing off the top of the envelope and emptying the contents onto the bed. Two one-dollar bills flutter out along with a quarter-sized medal. Jesus reads the part that says each bill offers "one dollar in silver payable to the bearer on demand." But Kid is more interested in the medal, holding it close to his face. "I think it's a saint," he says, showing it to Jesus who fails to identify the image as well.

On a hunch I tell Kid to get some baking powder out of the kitchen. When he comes back, I pour some into my hand and rub the medal in it until it shines bright. "Silver," I say. "And it's not a saint. It's the Sacred Heart." Though it's somewhat worn, I am sure I'm right, it is Jesus standing arms opened outward, exposing a sunburst core. On the back of the medal is the very thin remnant of a short engraving. I give it to Kid.

He reads. "We are happy here."

"I don't get it," I say. I can't keep holding back. "You're Chinese. The man in those letters is Filipino."

Kid and Jesus look at me with the same expression, as if I've just spoken a language they don't know. "I never said I'm Chinese," Kid says.

"But your last name is Yeung."

"I never said that either. That's my mother's maiden name. I'm both."

"Brother," Jesus says, "don't judge a neighbor by his cover."

If "helping" is to make me realize I'm an idiot, then Jesus is hitting his mark.

I'm cowed and thinking. We sit in the bedroom another two hours, Kid and Jesus speculating on his father's life and where "here" might be. I paint, though I've entirely given up on the idea that somehow my artichoke field is going to be something I can give Gloree. But I am compelled to finish it for myself. For that matter, I can't even be sure if it isn't complete as is, an exercise in silvery-green perspective. The sketches of Kid help me decide one thing, though. It only makes sense if I approach the work straight on, that is, like it appears from the window. So, that's what it is, a view from my window, and who cares? It sprays out like a leaf rake on a brown background. If it weren't for the distant Wong family farmhouse, and a hint of late-afternoon horizon, it may as well have been just that. And what it has been missing all this time is life, is Kid watering the artichokes, hose stretched across the road, mop of black hair, red shirt.

The television is on in the background the whole time. A cow has gotten loose from somewhere and is grazing in one of the nature corridors. "Done," I say. "Done." They look, Jesus smiling at me and nodding, as if he never had any doubt in me. Both of them come over to inspect my work and I'm surprisingly nervous. "Real good," Jesus says. "Brother, that's real good."

Kid is quiet. He tilts his head, turns toward the window, which now possesses nearly the same light as in the painting. "See. I don't look Chinese. I guess I wouldn't flip you off now."

Behind him, part of his father's life lies spread out on the bed, the medal gleaming on top of it all. "And what did you learn from all of that?"

"That my father was just a very old and interesting stranger."

"Mine too," Jesus says.

I'm disappointed for Kid that this is what his whole enterprise has yielded. "So it's a bust?" I ask

Kid shrugs. "I was hoping I'd figure out a way to help my mom be happier. But at least I have her and my brother . . . and you guys." He looks at me directly. "I feel like you have a grief box too somewhere."

"On the nose," Jesus says, and then pivots to the television. For some reason the cow is in full trot. I can just make out that it's about parallel to us in the Hollywood corridor. Set against the natural vegetation, the grayish brush and yellow grasses, she looks strange, black and white and cartoonish, too bellied and milk heavy for this setting.

"I've never seen a cow up close," Kid says.

"Me neither," I say. Goats at the petting zoo I've seen, sheep, a donkey, but never a cow, and I remember from all those years ago Pops's one unkept promise. We look at Jesus.

He laughs, patting me on the shoulder. "I specialize in lost sheep." Then he claps his hands together in inspiration. "You know what? I'm going to take you two to see a cow."

You had to be there.

We roll past the artichoke fields, past the Korean and Mexican bodegas, past and beneath jacarandas just out of flower, Jesus pushing while Kid speculates what the cow will look like up close, names her Valerie. When we arrive at the fence separating the corridor from the city, we see immediately that we've guessed right. Valerie is maybe a block away, black-and-white tail slapping at her haunches, a haze of insects swarming around her face as her lower jaw churns. I've seen bison at Yellowstone, but somehow none of them were as magnificent as this fugitive cow. This big-shouldered boulder, standing in the dusky vegetation, a camouflage pattern in the wrong shades. A confident goddess. This is how Valerie astounds me. A cow at graze doesn't need redemption. How does one cow?

It's the first time I've been off my porch since my accident, and I find the warmth of the sun at my back a strange and fresh sensation. Jesus stands next to Kid who is pressed up against the fence, his fingers clinging to the chain-link as if at any moment he might scramble up and over. The air here carries the scent of chaparral, something dusty and comforting, and though there is no wind, the moment is lightly percussive.

We observe Valerie for about an hour. It's not such a bad thing to be outside watching a cow on vacation from wherever she belongs. "Well, brothers," Jesus says, "was it worth the trip?" Kid offers an enthusiastic nod but does not look away from Valerie.

"It's something I can check off my life list," I say, though neither of them know how true this is. And maybe because I'm standing next to a man named Jesus, I entertain the idea of Heaven, of Pops up there asking God for a favor for his boy, if He might just take a second or two and let a cow loose in Hollywood. And probably God doesn't feel obligated to a full-grown man like me, but there's Kid and maybe He confuses him for the boy my father mentions. It's a fantasy, I know, but when I'm sure Jesus and Kid aren't looking, I wink at the afternoon sky.

We roll to a stop at Kid's house, Jesus behind the wheelchair, Kid standing at my side. I compliment Jesus on the fact he has pushed me the entire way. "Stamina, brother," he says, lifting dog tags from beneath his shirt. "The marines taught me that." It is just past twilight. Kid's mother is at work, still. Blue light from their television seems to bulge from the living room windows. Kid's brother is awake, probably sitting with the woman who takes care of him most days. "I'm not going to tell him I opened the box," Kid says, and he is smiling.

Out of reflex I look up to the lit window of my room where Kid's box sits on my bed, the contents replaced and retied with a blue ribbon, lid closed. And in that same room is the artichoke field with my little red version of Kid drying in the corner. I am feeling something I haven't felt for a long time. Today I finished a painting, I've seen a cow, and I am happy. How simple.

Jesus's eyes are bright even in the dim light. He is smiling and nodding like he can read my mind, his dog tags a silvery glow in the center of his chest. Kid is smiling too, and if I could stand outside our little trio right now I'm sure we look like we're all in on the same funny secret. Only Kid has caught this feeling by the tail at the right age and with much more time to enjoy it.

"Repeat after me," I say impulsively.

He looks at me, and there is trust in his eyes.

"I, Kid," I begin, "promise to do whatever it takes to be . . ." I pause because the next word is going to be "happy" and that seems too easy and not what I mean at all. I look to Jesus for help.

"You got it, brother," he says. "To be. That's all it is."

Kid raises a hand in oath and repeats, giggling. Without another word, he jogs up his walkway to the porch, and Jesus and I start toward my house. "Hey," Kid calls to us. We turn to find him grinning, his smile bright even in the dim light. Both his arms are extended, two middle fingers pointing skyward. I send a pair back and wink, waiting until he enters the house.

"He's going to make some guy a good boyfriend in ten or fifteen years," Jesus says.

I'm surprised. "You know about that?"

Jesus shrugs and pushes me toward my house. "He doesn't say too much. And it's not my place to do much more than listen. But he trusts me."

"He doesn't trust me?"

"Nobody trusts you. But we like you."

Silence. What do I do with that? To our left, the artichoke

fields seem to pulse, a dim blue against black. In a couple of weeks, with all the plants full-grown, the photographers will be parked up and down the street like they have every year for as long as Los Angeles can remember.

When we arrive at the front of my house it strikes me that my living room lights are on, and since I'm thinking about it, we shut them off before we left. Then a thick shadow moves across the front window and I understand that Auntie has returned.

When Jesus rolls me in the door, Auntie is sitting on the couch having tea. She looks as if she's just come in from church, pink dress buttoned nearly to the neck, hair perfectly pinned.

"Hello," I say, trying to sound as if I didn't know she'd ever gone.

Standing, Auntie approaches me and kisses me on the forehead. Apples. "You look good." She nods to Jesus and I introduce them, though she doesn't seem surprised by the pronunciation of his name.

"We've met I think," she says, "at church?"

"Yes we have, sister," Jesus says. With that, he walks to the side of the room where the bar stands.

"Nothing for me," I say.

He gives me a look as if I should know better. "Just getting my duffel bag. Gotta hit the road, brother. Provo calls."

"You're leaving?"

"It's time," he says, slinging the duffel over his shoulder. "Lots to do."

The announcement is so sudden I don't know how to react.

"What about that help you were going to give me? What happened to that?"

He is already at the door, but turns around and sets the duffel at his feet. Looking at me straight in the eyes, his own as steady and kind as any I've ever seen, he opens his arms wide like a magician showing he has nothing to hide. "I took you to see the cow."

"Yes, you did," I say. "Today I finally saw a cow. You're kind of a savior."

Jesus laughs. "Brother, you don't need no damn savior. What you need is a little less self-respect." His tone remains surprisingly friendly as he says this. "You got people around who care about you and you give them no consideration and your peak experience is watching a random-ass cow. That's some deep-seeded privilege right there. Like yourself less for a little while so you can like yourself more."

"Sermon on the Exit," I say.

He nods and raises his hand like Kid before his oath. "I, Thomas," he says, giving me the pistol-point gesture with his other hand. "You know the rest."

As I watch the door close it occurs to me that sometimes parts of our lives proceed like plays. Lately my house has felt like the stage set for a tragedy, or a really bad comedy, perhaps. And then, Jesus, my own deus ex machina.

"See," I say to Auntie, "you got your wish after all. I found Jesus."

Without missing a beat, she looks at me with forgiveness. "I'm sorry I gave up on you, Thomas." With that she collects herself almost instantly into a businesslike position, explaining that she really hadn't any intention of coming back, at least not for a long while. She tells me she hated seeing me every day and not trusting me and that she can't stand recognizing all the ways I've turned into my father. And then, as if she's done with that emotion, she springs the big news.

"So, when Gloree called and asked if I could let her in, I took it as a sign."

"Gloree was here? Today?"

"She said it was an emergency. Her client was having a dinner party and she needed the painting. She couldn't get ahold of you and wanted to come over and check if it was done."

"I'm in the doghouse," I say. I look at Auntie to practice the confession I'll have to give to Gloree, the one that will permanently drive her away. "I didn't finish her painting."

"It looked finished to me."

"What did?"

"The painting. I'm sure she loved it except that she said it wasn't fully dry."

Without explaining I roll myself as fast as I can to the bedroom door but I don't have to enter. The easel is empty. "Hell," I say.

Auntie is already behind me. "What's wrong?"

"Can you trust me," I say, "if I told you that right now I really need one drink? A double."

Not in the Cards

Now is the *now*. Before *this* is the then, and finally I've finished reading a new book, well, new to me but a lost classic I have no memory of purchasing, Yegor Sidorov's nineteenth-century novel *Valera's Scream*. Lots of landscape as seen from the windows of a Russian plantation, and a fear of art becoming actual currency. In response, Valera paints a woman who is in deep lament, a work that is found to be universally vulgar and repulsive, yet judged as undeniably perfect. It is an object that draws both rich and poor to Valera's salon, and like Mecca, has no price because no offer would ever dare be made. "The people still visit," Valera says, sitting as a very old man before the woman he painted so many years earlier. "They come because she needs them."

It's an autumn wedding, which in Los Angeles means Santa Ana winds off the desert and sun-bleached grasses that become expressways for wildfires. Still, Gloree insists on an outdoor ceremony, even though she said she'd never get married anywhere but a courthouse. People can change, and who am I to tell her no? For one thing, I'm not her groom. Still, Gloree makes an exceptional bride. She wears a knee-length denim dress with dungaree straps and an orange sapphire-studded veil matching the sapphire beauty she is marrying—red-haired Shanna, red hair that curls perfectly above the collar of her tux, hair that makes her a tall, upside-down exclamation mark with shiny red endpoint. She's beaming as Gloree walks down the aisle on my arm, sun on our cheeks, wind at our backs. I'm giving her away because I was drunk when I promised. My theory is that she knew when she asked, and knew, too, that I would keep my promise. So I sit in the section reserved for the bride's family, which is comprised of Auntie, me, and Gloree's mother, who watches sympathetically if not enthusiastically. Her husband emotionally relapsed, even now, misses Bennie with a husband in her future, and refused to attend.

My deal in promising to give Gloree away is that I will not attend the reception. When she protested, I confessed it was also my wedding gift. I would be no bonus to her if there was an open bar, if I even managed to head home largely sober, and then found myself T-boned at an intersection. "That is a very limited phobia, Tommy," Gloree said to me in response.

How did we get to the point where we could even have such a conversation? The catastrophic version wrote itself. Me, the near invalid watching religious television with his Auntie in a room filled with mostly unread books managed to finish one painting with a little help from Kid and Jesus. A poster of the whole thing would show a string of my footprints bordered by a couple more pairs on both the left and right. So while I was out watching Valerie the cow, Gloree took the painting of Kid and the artichoke field, and her client said yes and wrote a big fat check.

"I wasn't sure," Gloree confessed when she gave me my commission. "It didn't seem contemporary enough."

*

"Thomas," she whispers in my ear after the wedding, "are you really not going to be at the reception?" She has pulled me aside while the photographer stages some final photographs, cussing every gust of wind that musses hair and flips up skirts.

"I can't," I tell Gloree. "It's still day by day. The monkey isn't letting go of his riding crop so easy. Monkeys don't pray, but they whip."

She looks at me, not getting the reference, but softly acknowledging a truth in my response. "You'll be fine," she says.

"And besides." I laugh. "It was hard enough being in the wedding of the only woman I've ever loved."

Gloree waves off a plea from the photographer and patient Shanna, and I take one of her hands in mine. "That *was* love, Thomas. I promise."

"Yes, it was."

"And I still need you."

I kiss Gloree lightly on the forehead and pose for three or four blessedly quick photos with the wedding party before heading to the parking lot. At the sidewalk I'm confronted by a man in a blue silk shirt with two exquisitely groomed white poodles on silver leashes. "For the five o'clock," he says as he passes, clearly exasperated.

"Hey," I call, and he stops. I take out a couple of my new cards and hand him one. "Give this to the owner?" He takes it but hardly pauses, reading it as the poodles bobble along ahead of him. The card remaining in my hand feels surprisingly good. Even if it doesn't tell the whole story, clearly I've upgraded.

Dog Portraiture
By Tom Layton Wills
Immortalize Your Pet!
One Sitting, Fast Service

For a few seconds I watch the dogs that I might someday paint. They are headed past Gloree who is posing for a photograph next to the woman she needs more than me. Someday soon Gloree and Shanna will come over and I will serve them with a tea set gifted to me by Gloree's parents, a fact I have committed to memory. She will ask me what I'm working on, and I will show her, perhaps, a half-finished Pomeranian or schnauzer and nothing else, because there will be nothing else, not art, at least. I may even like myself a little more. But there will absolutely be no sadness because I will turn to the books I've most recently read and the stacks along the baseboards and I will say, "These, Gloree, I'm working on these." And Kid will be there, Auntie too with Jesus in her heart, people I need and who seem to need me. I am too far gone, too broken to be made new and I know it. I'll be in and out of rehab forever. But then, I think, if you are really trying, knowing that people need *you* is the kind of glue that can keep a person whole.

the wooden escalator

"Trust me. I've seen them operate it," the first boy said. They stood holding hands in just enough light to stare upward and into the length of modernity. Tomorrow, crowds would pour into the department store for a look at what had been called alternately a "civic menace," "Godless machinery," and, with cautious optimism, "the latest." The pair unclasped hands, the first boy disappearing into a dark corner, his translucent image replaced by the sound of hinges, and then a great hum followed by the rhythmic thudding of wood. The stairs were indeed moving. A wonder!

The two were side by side again with pinkie fingers clasped. The second boy stood on his toes at the excitement of such a gift. "I wish the lights were on. I wish I could see it." "Trust me," the first boy said. "It's an astonishment! They've turned oak into gold. Tomorrow, men in red linen suits with blue piping will stand at each end to assist the gentler sex."

"Aw," the second boy kidded, "you don't need assistance." If only there was better light he could have enjoyed the reaction.

"Shall we?" the first boy said. "Trust me?" He leaned and kissed the other on the cheek.

The second boy was hesitant at first, but stepped forward and ascended, followed quickly by the first boy, each, by fractions, disappearing into the dark elevation.

I was on watch that night. I let these boys have their fun, but of course I had to pursue. Only, when I reached the moving staircase, it was still, and I found no boys in the building that night. I swear they were there. I remember their almost silhouettes. The long breeches and suspenders. One of them wore a cap in the manner of a newsie. They were tender with each other. I saw them and wanted to follow. I did.

ande Books is a nonprofit independent literary press uartered in Louisville, Kentucky. Established in 1994 ampion poetry, fiction, and essay, we are committed ating lasting editions that honor exceptional writing. over two hundred titles in print, we have earned a ated readership and a national reputation as a publisher erse forms and innovative voices.

acknowledgments

Thank you to Brian Yost, handsome husband, Purdue University's Department of English, and Adam McOmber. Five books precede this new and selected, and the spirit and content of their acknowledgment pages are imported here. If you're there, you're here. Long ago, Sally Kim and PJ Mark read some of this book's fiction, then gave me a career. Thomas Alvarez gave me a life. Renee, Rebecca, Amy, Michele, Mike, Brittany, Gary, and Debbie, you didn't get to pick me, but thanks for sticking. Yee-shing Leung, if you didn't pursue your dreams in the United States, I couldn't have pursued mine. Catherine DiTomaso, you've proven that the warmest empires are built by love and loyalty.

Grateful acknowledgment is made to the following publications in which versions of these stories were first published:

Who's Yer Daddy: Gay Writers Celebrate Their Mentors and Forerunners: "The Seismology of Love and Letters: A Guide to the Ride?"

Velocity: "All the Presidents, Men"

The Rupture: "First It's a Lake, Then It's a River," "Fuzzling," and "Settlement"

Story: "Six Ways to Jump Off a Bridge" and "The Fish Is Gone. But Cake Is Here"

The Ocean State Review: "Undoing"

World Famous Love Acts: Stories: "Dog Sleep"

Always Crashing: "In Case of an Emergency, Are You Willing and Able to Perform the Following Functions?"

Good River Review: "Some Bones"

River City: "World-Famous Love Acts"

Hyphen: "Librarians on Ice"

BRIAN LEUNG, author of *All I Should* *of Thousands!*, *World Famous Love A* *Home*, is a past recipient of the La Outstanding Mid-Career Noveli the Asian American Literary A Sarabande Books Mary McCart fiction, creative nonfiction, and outlets like *Gulf Coast*, *Story*, *Th* *Review*, *Indiana Review*, and else University.

Sara
heac
to c
to c
Wit
dedi
of di

acknowledgments

Thank you to Brian Yost, handsome husband, Purdue University's Department of English, and Adam McOmber. Five books precede this new and selected, and the spirit and content of their acknowledgment pages are imported here. If you're there, you're here. Long ago, Sally Kim and PJ Mark read some of this book's fiction, then gave me a career. Thomas Alvarez gave me a life. Renee, Rebecca, Amy, Michele, Mike, Brittany, Gary, and Debbie, you didn't get to pick me, but thanks for sticking. Yee-shing Leung, if you didn't pursue your dreams in the United States, I couldn't have pursued mine. Catherine DiTomaso, you've proven that the warmest empires are built by love and loyalty.

Grateful acknowledgment is made to the following publications in which versions of these stories were first published:

Who's Yer Daddy: Gay Writers Celebrate Their Mentors and Forerunners: "The Seismology of Love and Letters: A Guide to the Ride?"

Velocity: "All the Presidents, Men"

The Rupture: "First It's a Lake, Then It's a River," "Fuzzling," and "Settlement"

Story: "Six Ways to Jump Off a Bridge" and "The Fish Is Gone. But Cake Is Here"

The Ocean State Review: "Undoing"

World Famous Love Acts: Stories: "Dog Sleep"

Always Crashing: "In Case of an Emergency, Are You Willing and Able to Perform the Following Functions?"

Good River Review: "Some Bones"

River City: "World-Famous Love Acts"

Hyphen: "Librarians on Ice"

Chardé Barrett Photography

BRIAN LEUNG, author of *All I Should Not Tell*, *Ivy vs. Dogg: With a Cast of Thousands!*, *World Famous Love Acts: Stories*, *Lost Men*, and *Take Me Home*, is a past recipient of the Lambda Literary Jim Duggins, PhD Outstanding Mid-Career Novelist Prize. Other honors include the Asian American Literary Award, WILLA Award, and the Sarabande Books Mary McCarthy Prize in Short Fiction. Brian's fiction, creative nonfiction, and poetry have appeared widely in outlets like *Gulf Coast*, *Story*, *The Barcelona Review*, *Crab Orchard Review*, *Indiana Review*, and elsewhere. He is a professor at Purdue University.

Sarabande Books is a nonprofit independent literary press headquartered in Louisville, Kentucky. Established in 1994 to champion poetry, fiction, and essay, we are committed to creating lasting editions that honor exceptional writing. With over two hundred titles in print, we have earned a dedicated readership and a national reputation as a publisher of diverse forms and innovative voices.